SPINETINGLERS

#30

SABER-TOOTHED TIGER

M. T. COFFIN

AN AVON CAMELOT BOOK

This is a work of fiction. Names, characters, places, and incidents either are the product of the author's imagination or are used fictitiously. Any resemblance to actual events, locales, organizations, or persons, living or dead, is entirely coincidental and beyond the intent of either the author or the publisher.

AVON BOOKS
A division of
The Hearst Corporation
1350 Avenue of the Americas
New York, New York 10019

Copyright © 1998 by Jim DeFelice
Published by arrangement with the author
Visit our website at http://www.AvonBooks.com
Library of Congress Catalog Card Number: 97-94043
ISBN: 0-380-79606-6
RL: 4.9

All rights reserved, which includes the right to reproduce this book or portions thereof in any form whatsoever except as provided by the U.S. Copyright Law. For information address Avon Books.

First Avon Camelot Printing: February 1998

CAMELOT TRADEMARK REG. U.S. PAT. OFF. AND IN OTHER COUNTRIES, MARCA REGISTRADA, HECHO EN U.S.A.

Printed in the U.S.A.

OPM 10 9 8 7 6 5 4 3 2 1

> If you purchased this book without a cover, you should be aware that this book is stolen property. It was reported as "unsold and destroyed" to the publisher, and neither the author nor the publisher has received any payment for this "stripped book."

1

I'm a saber-toothed tiger.

That's right. The big cat with ugly fangs and an appetite to match. The kind that eats raw flesh. Maybe even yours.

I wasn't always this way. Just a few months ago, I was a regular kid going to school, playing games, teasing my little sister. It was a heck of a lot of fun.

Then I found out there are more things going on in the world than anyone could ever think possible. Even in my wildest nightmare, I wouldn't have dreamt up some of the stuff I've seen these last few weeks.

Maybe if I tell my story, I can save someone from becoming tiger meat. If not—hey, I hear little kids are pretty tender.

* * *

It all started one Friday afternoon when I came home after school. Three cats were sitting on the split-rail fence I helped my dad put up last year. It runs along our property line, near the driveway. My dad said he wanted to put it there for show. It does look nice, but he also put it there to remind our neighbor, Mrs. Johnson, where her yard ended. Mrs. Johnson had a flower bed near there, and she was always piling old leaves and junk on our lawn. Growing grass was tough.

She won't do that any more.

As soon as I got off the bus that day, I noticed these three cats on the fence. Two were pretty big, but otherwise ordinary. One was gray, with stripes like a tiger. Another looked almost like a leopard, with orange-yellow fur and black spots. The last was puny. His brown hair stuck out from his face, sort of like a lynx's.

I'd never seen them before, but that didn't seem unusual at the time. We live in a subdivision that must have two or three hundred other houses. There are always some new pets coming around.

They usually don't hang around this end of the block too long. Mr. Walker across the street has a huge German shepherd named Sweetie Pie. His name really ought to be Killer. He's about the meanest dog going. Most afternoons Sweetie Pie is chained up around back, but every morning the Walkers tie him to the tree in the front yard. Whenever I wait for the bus he barks at me. It's as if he's saying, "The day I break this chain, you're breakfast."

Since this was the afternoon, the Walkers' dog was nowhere in sight. I figured that was a good thing for these cats. The two big ones looked kind of fat and lazy. They were probably used to an easy life. The little one could have been knocked over by a gust of wind.

Or so I thought.

I did notice one thing. Most cats, when I run down the driveway to the house, will run away. Not these bad boys. They sat there on the fence, watching me like traffic cops. I thought of waving my hands at them and yelling. I changed my mind. Something about the way they looked at me, well, it made me just a little uneasy.

Besides, I had a lot of stuff to do. My mom works as a secretary. Usually, she's home when I get home, but today she had to work late, until four o'clock. I was supposed to go inside and call her as soon as I got home.

First I hit the refrigerator for a quick snack. Mom had left a piece of apple pie. I wolfed it down and drained a glass of milk. Then I called my mom.

She said the usual—she loved me and I'd better

do my homework before I went out. Plus, I had to stay out of trouble and stay in the yard. I promised I would.

My little sister Dakota Rose goes to elementary school. She gets home at 3:30 P.M. Since mom was working late, I had to be there to meet her.

Even though we fought sometimes, I loved my little sister. Like last year, she was getting made fun of in school because of her name. She's named after an Indian tribe, because dad says there's Indian blood in our family. Anyway, this idiot third-grader was making fun of her. So he and I had a little chat. That straightened him right out.

I was always doing stuff like that. 'Cause she's my sister.

After getting off the phone, I did my math homework. Ms. Ferris had given us two pages of geometry problems to work on. The first two were tough, but the rest seemed to get easier as I went along. I was done in no time.

Before going outside, I took my lucky key chain out of my pocket. The lucky part was a stone that had strange markings on it. They looked a little like rounded triangles. Supposedly, Indians had made it a long time ago. Not as a key chain, of course. It had probably been part of a necklace or a belt or something, because there was a hole through the middle. My dad had given it to me when I was really little, and it had brought me good luck ever since. No matter where I went, I usually had it with me.

Grabbing a soda, I went to get my basketball from the garage. We have a hoop in the driveway. I figured I'd work on my shooting until Dakota came home.

As soon as I walked into the garage, I pulled the rope on the automatic door opener. Just as the motor started to whirl, I heard three strange voices. They sounded high-pitched and tinny, as if they were coming through a metal speaker. But what got my attention was what they were saying. I can't remember the exact words, but they were something like this:

"I think we ought to eat her."

"Yeah, she'll sure be tasty."

"What about the kid?"

"He's in the house. He'll never see us."

"We ought to eat him, too. He looked tender."

"Roast him! Roast him!"

Then the door began swinging upwards. It's totally automatic, and once it starts to open, there's no way to stop it. I stood right in the middle of the garage, petrified. I don't mind saying I was as scared as I have ever been. I thought I was going to die. I thought three ghouls would be right there, blood drooling from their mouths.

But there wasn't anyone in the driveway. No one was in sight.

No one, except those three cats.

For a second, I didn't know what to do. I couldn't believe that I had imagined the voices. They had seemed so real. Heck, they had to be real.

But there was no one there, at least not that I could see.

I bent down and put the soda on the floor. Then I took a deep breath, told myself not to worry, and took a step out of the garage.

It was a baby step, I admit. At any second, I expected to come face to face with some horrible ghoul. Getting turned into a kid burger isn't exactly my idea of after-school fun. But nothing happened.

I took another step out of the garage, then another and another. There was no one there.

In fact, the whole block seemed deserted. The only living things around were the cats.

Those cats. They were sitting on the fence, looking at me with their cat eyes.

"What are you looking at?" I said to them. "Why don't you go home? Mrs. Johnson will have a fit if you go in her garden. Scat!"

They just sat there like they didn't hear me. All right, I told myself, don't get mad at the stupid cats. They didn't do anything. You're just letting your imagination run wild. I picked up my basketball and started taking shots. I flubbed my first three, even the easy one right next to the basket. That was kind of disappointing. I tried concentrating harder, but I still couldn't get any of the balls to go in. I dribbled the ball at the foul line, trying to get into a steady rhythm. In my mind, I saw the ball swishing through the basket.

But nothing worked. By the time I took a break to drink my soda, I had gone zero for twenty-seven. The soda didn't help, either. When it was done, I fired up fourteen straight shots without a basket. And my fifteenth rebounded off the house and started rolling toward the road.

As I hurried after it, I heard some wise guy say, "Boy, that kid has to be about the worst basketball player ever. When he plays, it's not basketball. It's basket-bull."

I grabbed the ball and whirled around. I was mad. I don't like it when someone makes jokes about me, even if they're lame ones.

But again, there was no one there. Just those dumb cats, sitting on the fence.

Whoever was making fun of me didn't even have the guts to hang around. With no one else there to blame, I yelled at the cats.

"Go on, get! Run away! Yaahhhh!" I yelled.

Not that it did any good. They looked at me like I was nuts. Then they went back to licking their paws.

OK, I thought. Pretend I'm not here. I can play that game, too.

I went back to the foul line and took another shot at the basket. Only this time, I made sure I would miss—and that the rebound would head toward the fence where the cats were sitting.

Sure enough, it did. They ran clear around Mrs. Johnson's house.

I laughed and laughed. But when I went to get the ball on her lawn, I heard more voices.

"That kid's a brat."

"Forget about him. What about the old lady?"

"Let's eat her. I'm hungry."

I stood as still as a rock in a quarry pit. I told myself I must be imagining things. It was kind of windy, and the trees were rustling.

I bent down and picked up the ball. When I stood, I listened again.

There were no voices. I've been watching too many horror movies, I told myself.

But as I took a step toward my house, I heard a door slam. It sounded a lot like the back door to Mrs. Johnson's house.

Mrs. Johnson wasn't my favorite person in the world. Mom said we should be nice to her because her husband had died the year before. But she didn't make it easy. She was a nut about her garden. Anytime a basketball or a baseball came within ten feet of it, she'd yell. And she was always coming over to our yard to tell me about a report I should write for school. See, Mrs. Johnson is the town historian. She thinks she knows everything about Wappinoe, which is where we live. She would pester me about the Indians who used to live here, or the Civil War soldiers who came from nearby. I like history, but her stories were about as exciting as watching asphalt turn gray.

Even so, I didn't want to see her eaten. Of course, I didn't exactly want to be eaten myself. But someone had to warn her. I took a deep breath, then ran to the front door. As I pressed the buzzer, I set my legs for a quick escape.

I heard noises inside the house.

"Mrs. Johnson, Mrs. Johnson!" I shouted. "Hurry!"

"I'm coming. Wait a second!"

Hearing her voice made me relax—but not too much. "Mrs. Johnson, hurry! It's important!"

"All right," she said. I could hear her footsteps just inside the door. The doorknob twisted and the door sprung open.

Revealing a green ghoul of a monster, who leered at me with a hungry smile.

I ran from that front yard so fast, I must have created a sonic boom.

Even so, I could hear footsteps behind me. Whatever had answered Mrs. Johnson's door was out for blood—mine.

As luck would have it, my sister's school bus was heading down the block toward our house. I had never been so glad to see a school bus in my life. I waved my hands and ran for it, practically knocking over my sister as she got off.

"Gee, Alan," she told me as I struggled to catch my breath. "How come you're so glad to see me?"

"Get back on the bus, quick!" I put my hand on the door to keep the driver from closing it.

"Are you crazy? It's Friday. I'm done with school for the week."

"No, no, you don't understand," I shouted. "Look, it's coming to get us."

"What? Mrs. Johnson?" she asked.

I turned back. Sure enough, the "thing" that had been chasing me was Mrs. Johnson. She was walking down the road, wiping her face with a big towel that had green goop all over it.

"Alan, I'm sorry I scared you, honey," she said.

That was another thing I hated about Mrs. Johnson—she always called me "honey."

"I had my face covered with a new mud treatment," she explained. "I was going to take it off before answering the door, but you made it sound like an emergency. I'm sorry that it was so scary."

The driver looked down from inside the bus. "Say, kids, is everything all right? I'm not leaving you off here, Dakota Rose, if there's a problem. You're Alan, right? Are you OK?"

I nodded. Really, I felt like Mr. Number One Fool. Who wouldn't? Scared by green mud! A new low. I felt so embarrassed and confused I couldn't even talk. All I could do was follow Dakota Rose back to our house. Mrs. Johnson came, too. She kept apologizing.

"It's all right," I told her finally. "I wasn't really scared."

I don't know if she believed me or not, but she finally went back to her house. We went inside ours. I helped my sister with her homework—it was pretty easy stuff, since she's only in first grade. Pretty soon, Mom came home and I forgot all about the mud, the voices and everything else.

We had meat loaf for dinner that night. It was smothered with tomato sauce and tasted so good I had three pieces.

Maybe that's why I didn't sleep all that well. Maybe that's why I had strange dreams.

I'm not sure how to describe them. Usually when I have a dream, it's like a movie or a TV show. There's a beginning, a middle, and an end, unless I wake up. But these were just like weird pictures flashing through my brain:

Green-faced ghouls. Cats that could grow teeth a foot long, like daggers. People turning into monsters and animals.

Not exactly the kind of stuff that leaves you feeling rested in the morning.

Still, Saturday didn't start off that badly. In the morning I went to Little League, where I had a home run and a double. I also managed to make a great catch in left field. We ended up winning 10-7.

When I got home, it was almost dinner time. My dad was just debating whether to start up the barbecue.

That's when Mom suggested inviting Mrs. Johnson over.

My father frowned. She wasn't his favorite person, either.

"It will mean a lot to her if we invite her over," said Mom. "She doesn't have that many friends nearby. Besides, we have plenty of chicken in the refrigerator."

Mom went to call Mrs. Johnson while Dad and I went to set up the grill. It's an old-fashioned kind with charcoal. Lighting it can be pretty tricky. Dad had just gotten it going pretty good when Mom came out the back door.

"This is a bit odd," she said. "I called but no one answered."

"Maybe she went somewhere," my dad suggested.

"No, her car's in the driveway. I'm a little worried. Maybe we should go over and see."

"She's probably just taking a nap," said my father. "Let's leave her be."

"Alan, go run next door and ring her bell."

"Me?"

"Yes," said my mom. "Go on. If you wake her up, apologize."

I started to protest, but then I saw a look cross my mom's face. It was the kind of look that means, *Get going—now! Or no dessert.*

So I went. I'd be lying if I said I wasn't thinking about what had happened the day before. But I knew it was silly. I shook my head just thinking about it. Ghouls! Eating people! Come on!

If such things really did exist, the last person they would eat would be Mrs. Johnson. She was all skin and bones.

Even so, my heart started pounding as I approached the door. I hesitated before ringing the bell.

I couldn't hear anything inside. No footsteps, nothing. I waited a few seconds, then I rang the bell.

Nothing. When no one answered a second time, I leaned on the bell, making it ring for about ten seconds straight.

The house was as quiet as a tomb.

I put my face on the window next to the door, trying to see inside. It took a second for my eyes to adjust to the light and glare. When they did, I saw that Mrs. Johnson's living room was a mess. Books and papers were scattered on the floor. That wasn't like her at all.

And Mrs. Johnson wasn't anywhere to be seen.

As I pushed closer to the glass for a better view, the front door creaked open. It hadn't even been locked.

All of a sudden I felt tingly all over. It was

as if I had slept the wrong way on every part of my body.

"Mrs. Johnson?" I called.

There was no answer.

The door creaked open another inch.

It was probably the wind. Whatever—I flew back to my house and told Mom and Dad about the mess and the books being on the floor.

"We'd better investigate," said my dad.

"Don't you think we should call the police?" I asked. For a second I almost told him about the strange voices I'd heard, or thought I'd heard, the day before.

"Well, I don't know if we should call the police just yet," my father said. "Let's check on the house first. Maybe she just went for a walk and forgot to lock up. I've done that myself plenty of times."

"But the living room is a mess," I said. "Like there was a fight or something."

"Let's take a look."

My mom called over there one last time, just to make sure. Then she got my sister and all four of us went to Mrs. Johnson's house.

The first thing my dad did was push the door wide open. "Anybody home?" he shouted.

"Maybe she's taking a nap," said my mom.

"Hell-o! Anyone here?" said my father, much louder.

No one answered.

"This isn't like Linda," said my dad, taking a step into the living room. "Books and papers all over the floor? She's a neat freak."

"The bookcase fell over," said my mom, pointing. "That's what the problem is."

"I see," said dad. He walked over and picked it up. "Still, why didn't she fix it?"

"Maybe it was too heavy for her," said my mom. "She *is* an old lady."

"She's not that old," said my dad. "This bookcase is light. Alan, pile the books up neatly while I look through the house. Maybe she fell and can't get up." He glanced at me, then called Mrs. Johnson by her first name. "Linda! Linda, are you there? Linda? Is anything wrong? Linda?"

As my dad disappeared into the kitchen, Dakota and I began picking up the books and magazines from the floor. Before the pile was more than a foot high, I realized something very strange.

There was cat hair all over the place—gray, orange, and brown.

And Mrs. Johnson was allergic to cats.

4

"Alan, what are you staring at?" asked my mom.

"This is cat hair," I blurted out.

"So?"

"Mrs. Johnson doesn't have cats. She told me and Dakota she's allergic, just like you. Remember, Dakota?"

"That's right," said my sister.

My mother came over and examined the fluffs of hair. "I don't think it's cat hair," she said. "Most of this looks too thick for a cat. It might have come from a sweater or a blanket."

"No, it's cat hair," I insisted.

"Du-huh," said Dakota. "It's not."

Little sisters.

Just then, my dad returned from the back of the house.

"See anything?"

"No sign of her. Her bed hasn't been slept in,

and everything's neat as a pin in the kitchen, except for some spilt milk."

"Milk?" I asked.

"There's an empty carton on the floor. There are a few dried drops near it. Either it was empty when it fell, or someone cleaned it up."

Cleaned it up, I wondered—or licked it up?

"Look at this, Dad. Cat hair."

My father examined the hair. "Nah. Mrs. Johnson doesn't have cats."

"But it's got to be cat hair, Dad."

My father gave me a strange look, then shrugged. "Whatever it is, it's not helping us now. I'm going to check the rest of the house," he told my mom. "Maybe you ought to call the police, just in case. It seems odd that her car would still be here. I'll check her room upstairs, where she keeps all the town history stuff."

Mom and Dakota left to call the police. I piled up the rest of the books while my dad went upstairs. I'm not sure why or how I knew that the cats I had seen yesterday were involved in this mystery, but I did. Maybe they belonged to whoever had done this, I thought.

Upstairs, my father tried to step lightly, as if he were tiptoeing through a minefield. Mrs. Johnson kept a lot of junk that wouldn't fit in the small museum at the town hall in her second-floor room. She once showed me a moose head up there. But mostly there were boxes and boxes of papers and old newspapers, nothing cool like swords or a cannon.

As I listened to my dad tiptoe around the clutter, I heard something else. Something that was much louder. It sounded like something being dropped and dragged. It seemed to come from the back of the house.

I don't know what it was that made me want to investigate. It wasn't courage—more like stupidity.

Holding my breath, I walked toward the hallway on the other side of the stairs. It led to Mrs. Johnson's bedroom, and then to the back of the house. The front door was open behind me. I crouched down as I reached the corner, and peered inside.

The hall was empty. The bedroom was about halfway down it on the right. At the end of the hallway on the left, there was another short hall. That went to the kitchen and the dining room.

I listened carefully, but I couldn't hear anything. I took a timid step into the corridor. When I realized the sound hadn't come from there, I relaxed a little. I thought maybe it was the wind. Or maybe my hearing was going whacko.

Still, I had to investigate just to be sure. I

wanted to prove I had nothing to fear. Pushing myself against the wall, I eased toward the bedroom doorway. Even though it was a bright sunny day outside, the light in there wasn't the best. I told myself that the bedroom was empty. I knew it had to be, since my dad had checked it out before.

Even so, I moved carefully, and dropped to the floor before I peeked through the doorway. Somewhere I read that if you're going to spy on someone, it's best to do it from the ground, where they're not expecting you to be. So that's what I did.

The room was empty. I stood up, laughing a little to myself. Nothing to be afraid of, I thought. I probably just heard my dad upstairs and got confused.

That's when I heard a thumping noise. I could tell it didn't come from upstairs.

The back hall? The kitchen?

I turned quickly and went out of the room. I stood in the hall for a moment, barely breathing. I didn't hear anything else.

If there had been a sound, it must have come from the back of the house. Either the hallway, or the dining room, or the kitchen.

Was I brave enough to investigate for myself?

Yes, I said silently.

I took a step forward.

It was my imagination, I insisted. Just my imagination.

The hallway was clear. The dining room and the kitchen were empty, just as my father had said they were. I sighed—and as soon as I sighed, I heard the noise again. It wasn't very loud, but it was steady. Every few seconds—thump-thump. Thump-thump.

Like a slow heartbeat.

Finally I realized where it was coming from—downstairs. The cellar door in the corner of the kitchen was ajar.

My father hadn't checked down there. All my courage vanished. I stared at the plain white door. My feet could have been welded to the floor. At any second, I expected some monster to come crashing out. I would scream, but it would be too late.

Then something grabbed me on the shoulder, and I screamed for real.

"Alan, calm down."

I nearly fainted before I realized it was only my dad.

"I didn't mean to scare you. Are you OK?"

I nodded. My voice had gone into hiding somewhere deep in my chest.

"I'm going to go check the cellar," said my father. "Wait here."

"I-I heard something down th-there," I struggled to say.

"What did you hear?"

"N-noise. Thumps. Like a heartbeat, maybe."

"OK. Just wait here."

But I didn't. I couldn't. No way. I started walking right behind him, down the steps.

There was another thump-thump.

"Sshh," said my father, turning and holding his finger in front of his mouth.

"It wasn't me," I hissed.

"Didn't I say wait for me upstairs?"

"I don't want to be alone," I admitted.

"All right. Stay here on the steps. And be quiet."

My father started back down the stairs. That's my dad—not afraid of anything.

Me, I'm petrified of my own shadow sometimes.

But that wasn't my shadow at the bottom of the stairs.

It looked like—a giant cat.

"Dad, no!" I screamed. "Wait!"

But it was too late—he reached the final step and turned to the right, exactly in the direction of whatever had cast the shadow.

5

"Alan, you're as jumpy as a mouse. Calm down." My dad scowled at me from the foot of the stairs.

"B-but—the shadow."

"What shadow?"

"Look. On the ground. It's a cat, dad. And I found cat hair upstairs, and yesterday—"

"That's not a cat." My dad shook his head. "Come here."

The three steps to the bottom of the stairs were about the longest steps I took in my life. My dad gripped me by the shoulder and turned me toward the shadow's origin. I closed my eyes, then opened them, not knowing what to expect.

Clothes. Hanging on a wooden drying rack.

"See?" said my dad. "There's nothing here but laundry."

"B-but the noise I heard?"

"That fan over there. Every few seconds it hits the sheets. See?"

He was right. Mrs. Johnson had left the sheets out to dry. There was an old-fashioned fan that moved back and forth. When it hit against the sheets, it made a sound similar to the one I had heard. Thump-thump.

Cats! Ghouls! I was letting my imagination run wild. All because of a fan and a clothesline.

We walked through the cellar. I have to admit, a couple of times my stomach curled up like a twisted rope—I was still plenty scared—but there was nothing there.

"Well, she's not in the house," said my dad, when we returned to the living room. "It's a mystery."

"I'm sorry I got so scared," I told him.

"Oh, don't worry about that," he said, tussling my hair. That's a bad habit of his I could never seem to break. "I was scared myself. The important thing is not to let fear paralyze you. 'Paralyze' means that you freeze, and you don't do something that you want to do."

I guess my dad's advice was pretty good. After all, if you turned to ice every time you were scared of doing something, you'd never get anywhere. The first time I went to ride a bicycle without training wheels, I was paralyzed, even though I didn't know what the word meant then. I could hardly even move. But my dad said not to worry. He would catch me if I fell. He did, too. It took a couple of weeks before I could ride on my own. And then one day I made a huge discovery. I was riding, and a curb came out of nowhere and smacked my wheel sideways. Well, all right, the curb was there and I wasn't paying attention. Same thing, more or less. Anyway, I went flying. But it didn't really hurt that much when I landed. I got a couple of bruises and some scrapes, and it was a good thing I had my helmet on. I'm not saying I liked it. But I learned that sometimes a couple of scrapes and bruises aren't that bad.

This wasn't the same thing, of course. This was a real mystery. Still, there was nothing to panic over.

Not yet, anyway.

The police arrived a short time after we returned to the living room. There were two officers, one a short guy barely bigger than me, and the other a woman who was taller than my dad. They searched the house the same as we had, and then asked us all sorts of questions.

It turned out that Dakota and I were the last ones who had seen Mrs. Johnson. I told the cops how she had come out of the house yesterday with her mud pack on, though I didn't say why she came running out.

"You're sure it was her?" asked the short policeman. He had a nose that looked a little like the tip of an ice-cream cone. Even though he was short, his voice was very deep. It reminded me of a tuba.

"It was definitely her," I said.

"Did you notice anything strange about her, or about the neighborhood yesterday?" asked the woman police officer.

"Well, there was one thing," I said. "Did you see all the cat hair in the house?"

"Cat hair?"

"Mrs. Johnson doesn't have a cat," I explained. "And yesterday, I saw three strange cats hanging around in her yard. Plus, there was an empty carton of milk on the kitchen floor."

"Cats?" laughed the short policeman. "You think a cat came and kidnapped her, kid?"

I could feel my face turn red hot.

"No," I said. "But maybe they were with someone who did."

The cop chuckled.

"Was there something else? Anything?" asked the other cop in a much nicer voice.

"Well, I heard—I thought I heard—voices. I couldn't tell where they were coming from. They said weird stuff, like, 'Let's eat the lady.' I thought they were talking about Mrs. Johnson."

"Let's eat the lady?" The short policeman laughed so hard I thought he was going to burst.

Man, I didn't like him one bit.

"I heard something weird," I insisted. "But the only people around when I looked were the cats."

"Cats aren't people, kid," said the male cop. He shook his head. "Boy, talk about an imagination."

"Just a second, Pete," said the lady cop. "Maybe something weird did happen here. You don't think the neighbor just disappeared and left her car, do you? And no woman would go somewhere and leave her pocketbook."

"Come on. You've never left the house and forgotten to take something? She probably got a ride to the mall with a friend," said her partner. "There are no signs of forced entry. Nothing seems out of place to me."

"The bookcase was knocked over," she insisted. I read her nameplate. It said Officer McAvery.

"The bookcase looks pretty flimsy," said the other cop. "Ten bucks says she knocked into it on her way out, and decided to take care of it when she got home. My bet is, she shows up in ten minutes with a ton of shopping bags under her arm." He started walking toward the front door.

"And you, kid—stop watching so much TV. Sheeze."

Most cops I like. My uncle Mike's a cop, and he's a real nice guy. But this one was a Class A jerk—a "wise apple" as my mom would say. I was glad to see him leave.

True, it didn't make sense that cats had attacked Mrs. Johnson, or been with someone who did. Cats aren't like dogs. They don't hang around for stuff like that. And I have to admit, this wasn't exactly the kind of neighborhood where your average, flesh-eating ghoul prowls for kicks. But there was no reason for him to laugh at me.

Officer McAvery asked my mom and dad a few more questions, then gave them a card with her number on it. She asked them to call if Mrs. Johnson showed up.

"Someone has to be missing for forty-eight hours before we can open a missing persons case," she explained. "Since Alan saw Mrs. Johnson yesterday afternoon, we'll open the case tomorrow if she's not back. Don't mind my partner," she added, looking at me. "He's been wrong before. You were right to tell me what you thought you heard."

What I *thought* I heard. Even the nice cop didn't believe me.

As I walked back to our house, I admitted to myself how silly the whole thing sounded. Three little pussy cats had eaten my neighbor?

It wasn't a story even Dakota Rose would believe.

Not yet, anyway.

Mrs. Johnson didn't show up over the rest of the weekend. My mom talked to the police Sunday and again Monday morning; they said they would put out an alert. That meant other police would keep an eye out for her. They also said they would contact her relatives.

My mother also talked to a few other neighbors. No one remembered seeing Mrs. Johnson after I did. Nobody else remembered the cats. Mom said that Mrs. Johnson must have gone on a trip and forgotten to mention it.

She did go on trips, I had to admit. My mom had a key so she could water the plants when Mrs. Johnson was away. She went over and did that Sunday afternoon. Everything was exactly the way we left it, she said.

At school Monday morning our science teacher Mr. Elwell demonstrated how hot air is lighter than cold air. A friend of his owned a hot air balloon. He brought it in his pickup truck to the baseball field behind the school. Every kid in the class got to go up for a short flight. Five kids at a time crowded into the basket with Mr. Elwell and his pal Bob. The basket reminded me a little of the basket on the balloon at the end of *The Wizard of Oz*. Bob would turn a valve overhead, and flames would shoot into the balloon. The flames warmed the air. Up we went. He turned off the fire and we came back down. Hot air rises. Cold air descends.

It was so much fun I had totally forgotten the cats and Mrs. Johnson when I hopped off the bus that afternoon.

Which explains my shock when I saw that the three strange cats were back. And this time, they weren't on the fence—they were sitting at the edge of my driveway, licking their paws.

The bus roared away and left me standing at the edge of the street. Part of me wanted to run away. Another part thought I was just being silly, like the short cop had said.

I remembered my dad's advice about not being paralyzed. Easy to say, tougher to do. But I couldn't stand there all day. Slowly, I edged onto the lawn, toward the front door. My mom was inside the house. Even if these cats were up to something bad—and I wasn't sure they were—I ought to be able to get by them and get inside.

One step, two steps. Nothing happened. Then I took a third and felt myself tumbling to the ground.

I had forgotten about the lawn sprinklers.

I swore I heard snickers. I looked up quickly, but there was no one there. Only the cats, and they didn't seem to be paying attention. But I wasn't taking any chances—I jumped to my feet and started running for the door.

I was just about to reach the stoop when I realized my backpack was still lying on the lawn where I had fallen.

There was nothing to do but go back and grab it.

Filled with dread, I stopped in my tracks. I hesitated for a second, scared to turn around.

When I finally did, I saw that the cats were still sitting at the edge of the driveway like before. They hardly seemed to notice me.

Come on, I told myself. These are just three dumb cats. Two fatties and one runt. They can't hurt you. And they couldn't have done anything to Mrs. Johnson. You're letting your imagination run wild.

With a big sigh, I walked back to my pack. I

went slowly, trying to seem confident and brave—trying to *be* confident and brave.

"Boy, what a dumb kid," I heard as I bent to grab my backpack.

"Yeah. He's a loser. Trips over his own feet. Reminds me of a mouse I ate a few weeks back."

That got my attention, all right. I snapped up my pack and looked straight at the cats.

I took a quick glance around but didn't see anyone else. A little nervous, I reached into my pocket for my key chain and good luck charm. Touching the stone made me feel more confident. You can't have too much luck at a time like this.

"What are you cats looking at, anyway?" I demanded.

For a second, nothing happened. Then the striped gray glanced at his two buddies and uttered a short "meow."

It wasn't anything I hadn't heard a million times before. It sounded a lot like the mew a kitten might make when it wanted to be fed.

An innocent little meow. No evil in that.

But it made my legs shake. Somehow I managed to take a step backwards, then another. The cats didn't move, and they didn't say anything—not meow, not boo.

OK, I thought to myself. Now I'm just scaring myself with silly nonsense. Cats don't talk. I'm going inside and doing my homework, and then I'm coming out to play basketball.

I turned around and took three or four nonchalant steps toward the front of the house. As I reached the narrow strip of flowers that separated the lawn from the front walk, I turned around.

The cats weren't in the driveway anymore. They were walking toward me on the lawn, tails up, noses twitching.

"He suspects something," snarled the brown cat. I saw his mouth move as I heard the words.

I bolted inside.

"Alan, didn't I tell you to go easy with that door?" demanded my mother after I slammed it shut behind me. She was standing in the front hallway. "What are you doing?"

"The cats," I managed. "They're right outside."

"What cats?"

"Don't open the door, Mom! They're the ones who ate Mrs. Johnson."

"Oh, don't be ridiculous. Cats don't eat people."

She took hold of the doorknob. I grabbed her.

"Let go of my arm," she said. Before I could stop her, my mom swung open the front door. I threw my arms up in front of my face, sure we were about to be attacked.

36

"Alan, what cats? What are you talking about?"

Sure enough, there were no cats at the door. In fact, there weren't any in the front yard, or in Mrs. Johnson's front yard either.

"Did something happen at school today?" my mom asked. "Was Steve Roberts picking on you again?"

Steve Roberts was an older kid who rode my bus. He started pushing me around during the winter because I wouldn't give him the dessert that came with my lunch. We got into a huge fight one day in the lunchroom, and both of us got in big trouble. We were sent up to the principal's office. It was a major hassle, with our moms coming to pick us up. I got grounded for a week.

Steve Roberts and I weren't exactly best friends now, but after the fight he mostly left me alone. He usually sat a few rows behind me on the bus coming home. Every so often, he'd say something stupid. Sometimes I'd say something back, but most times I'd just roll my eyes. Most other kids on the bus thought he was a jerk, too.

"Mom, I swear there were cats following me. Did the police find out anything new about Mrs. Johnson?"

"No. They do have a theory, though. They think she went with her sister on a cruise."

"A cruise?"

"Her sister in North Carolina left for a cruise this past Saturday morning, the day after you saw her. The sister's neighbors think she mentioned something about going with her sister."

"But Mrs. Johnson's car is still in the driveway."

"Grandma and Grandpa had a limousine pick them up when they flew to Hawaii, remember?" said my mom. "Maybe Mrs. Johnson did the same thing. Come on—how would you like some ice cream for a snack?"

I followed my mother into the kitchen. I wanted to believe what she was saying—it made sense logically. But something inside me wouldn't go for it. I knew I had heard those cats talking. I was convinced they were to blame for Mrs. Johnson's disappearance. The voices I had heard Friday afternoon had sounded exactly like the voices I had just heard coming from the cats.

It wasn't until I was doing my homework that I thought about ventriloquism. Someone who does ventriloquism can make it seem like someone or something else is talking. People who do that are called ventriloquists. Often they make puppets seem to speak. Their acts can be very funny.

It was the only logical explanation. But if it had been a ventriloquist, where had he been hiding? And since I had heard three different voices, did that mean there were three ventriloquists? And what about the cats? Where had they come from? Were they part of his act? Or just a coincidence?

I had a lot of questions, and not a lot of answers. One good thing did come from all of this, however—it gave me an excellent idea for my English homework. We had been assigned to write a story for class. I started to work on it while I ate my snack at the kitchen table. I imagined what it might be like if I were a ventriloquist, and I wanted to play a trick on a friend. Before I knew it, I had three pages written.

"I must say, you've been busy," said Mom, when she came into the kitchen an hour later to start dinner. "What are you working on?"

"A story for English class. Want to read it?"

"Sure. What's it called?"

" 'The Mad Ventriloquist,' " I said.

" 'The Mad Ventriloquist'?"

"Yup. It's about this kid who learns how to throw his voice. He scares the whole neighborhood, see, until the police come and lock him up. Then he manages to escape by throwing his voice in court."

"You have some imagination," said my mom, picking up the paper. "Where did you learn to spell ventriloquist?"

"I guessed."

"Well, you guessed right. But next time, use a dictionary just to be sure."

My mom liked the story mostly, except for the part where the ventriloquist tricks his mother into thinking that he's in his room when she punishes him. She corrected a few mistakes and I took it upstairs to re-write it on fresh composition paper. As I entered my room, I heard a peculiar noise, like something clawing at the window.

A curtain hung in front of the window, so I couldn't see what it was.

I was determined not to let my imagination get the better of me anymore. There was a tree right outside my window, and the noise could have been made by a tree branch rubbing up against the glass. I strode toward the window and grabbed the drape, yanking it back out of the way.

The gray tiger-cat hissed at me from outside the glass. I fell back on the bed, so scared I was in shock.

"Alan, Alan, put your homework away for now and come and eat dinner! Come on. You've been in your room for an hour at least. Alan?"

I'd been there for an hour, all right, but I hadn't been doing my homework. I had been lying on my back in the middle of my bed, too scared to even move. I remembered what my dad told me about not being paralyzed. Ha! I was so scared I don't know how my lungs even managed to breathe.

"Alan? Are you OK?"

I looked over and saw my father in the middle of the doorway.

"Y-yes," I squeaked.

"What happened? Did you fall asleep?"

Honestly, I didn't know what to say. How could I tell my father that I had been scared out of my wits by a cat?

A cat that had eaten my next-door neighbor.

"Dad, could you do me a favor?" I asked, sitting up.

"Sure, pal, if it's legal."

I laughed. Dad was always saying stuff like that. I began to feel a little better, or at least less scared.

"Could you check the window? I thought I heard something out there."

"You're not letting your imagination run wild again, are you?" he asked.

"No. But if you could just check, I'd feel better."

"No problem, buddy." He went over to the drapes. He pulled them back all the way, looked around—then opened the window.

"Doesn't seem to be anything here," he said, sticking his whole head and arms outside.

I was just getting off the bed when he shouted, "Except for this!"

I screamed and fell back against the wall, expecting to see my dad devoured by a hideous cat beast. I imagined all sorts of horrible stuff—until he turned his hand toward me so I could see. In it was a gross, misshapen green blob.

Alien space slime? Snot from a ten-foot tall monster? A killer maggot looking for supper?

Not exactly.

"Looks like you hid some Halloween candy in the gutter, then forgot about it," said my dad, holding out the plastic baggie.

Talk about gross. He was right. I had put it out there months and months ago because Dakota Rose was snooping around for my chocolate.

"Here, take it," said my dad. "It's not going to bite you. Though I wouldn't be surprised if there is something alive in there."

I took the baggie and headed for the kitchen garbage pail. Mom intercepted me.

"Oh, yuk," she said. "Outside with that—throw it directly in the trash outside. Do not pass Go, do not collect two hundred dollars."

"But Mom—"

"Out! It's toxic."

I held the slimy bag of corroded candy bars as far from my body as possible as I headed out the back door for the garbage pail. Even though the putrid pus was on the inside of the plastic bag, I couldn't help but feel a little sick to my stomach.

I kept my head down as I walked, trying to hold my breath. As I reached for the garbage cover lid, I realized there was something sitting on the ground right next to the can.

The striped gray cat.

With a start I threw the baggie up in the air.

The cat took a step toward me. In the next moment, the baggie with its radioactive sludge fell right in front of him. He shot away like a bullet.

I didn't hang around to watch. I was too busy hightailing it back into the house.

7

Needless to say, I didn't have much of an appetite after that. I sat down at my place in the kitchen and blinked at my food. Usually I love fluffy mashed potatoes, but the white swirls reminded me of the tufts of cat hair I had seen at Mrs. Johnson's. The breaded chicken cutlets Mom served up looked like flattened pieces of fried mice.

And the green peas—I don't want to talk about it!

I was pretty out of it. When my sister knocked her milk over into her dish, I didn't even laugh.

I still had a full plate when everyone else was cleaning up. My dad asked if something was wrong. I didn't know what to say. That I had been spooked by a cat? All I could do was shrug and ask to be excused.

It took a long time to re-write my composition

homework upstairs. Every time I finished a sentence, I looked over my shoulder at the window. A couple of times I thought I heard scratching, but saw nothing. I can't even guess how often I crept over to the window to make sure it was still locked tight.

When I'd finished, I went downstairs and watched TV with my family. The shows were dumb, but I watched anyway. Part of me was afraid something weird was going to happen.

Another part of me wanted something weird to happen. I don't know how to explain it. I wasn't rooting for the three cats to come bursting through the front door and attack us. But if that happened, my fears would be proven correct. I'd know I wasn't going nuts.

That didn't happen. Bedtime came. I wheedled an extra ten minutes out of Mom, and then Dad said, "Up with you."

"How about you read me a story?" I asked.

"A bedtime story?" answered my dad. "Read one yourself."

"You should," Mom told Dad. "Go ahead. You haven't done that for years."

"Oh, why not?" said my father, leading me upstairs. "There's nothing on TV anyway."

It wasn't really a bedtime story I wanted. I was scared that something was waiting in my bedroom for me. I wanted my dad with me just in case.

I could tell as soon as he walked in that there was nothing there. I brushed my teeth, put on my Chicago White Sox pajamas and ducked under the sheets. Then, as my father was looking for a book on my shelf to read, I pretended to be falling asleep. I told him I was tired and he could read another night.

"You sure are acting strange lately," he said, turning off the light as he left.

I kind of wished he had left the light on.

When I finally drifted off to sleep, I had the worst nightmares I'd ever had.

The cats were there. All three of them, ten times bigger than in real life. And instead of cat faces, they wore hideous masks, with blood dripping from their lips. They growled and purred, and I understood I was going to be their next victim.

Then all of a sudden, it wasn't a dream. They circled the bed, growling and spitting. I was scared—petrified. But I remembered what Dad had said. I knew I had to do something.

"I'm on to you," I told them. "I know what you did to poor Mrs. Johnson. I'm calling the police as soon as I wake up!"

That's when the ring leader, the gray tiger-cat,

bolted onto the bed and jumped on my chest. I screamed as loud as I ever had in my life.

"Alan, are you having a nightmare?"
I opened my eyes and realized it had only been a dream. My mom was standing over my bed. It was morning.
"Oh—hi, Mom."
"Are you OK?"
"Perfect."
She gave me a funny look. "Come on, you're going to be late for the bus," she said. "Listen, I have to work late this afternoon, so I won't be here when you get home. Is that all right?"
"Sure," I told her. "Why wouldn't it be?"
"I don't know," she said, in a worried-mom kind of voice. "That was some scream you woke up with."
"I'm OK."
"You have to stop letting things bother you so much," she said. "Are you sure there's nothing wrong in school?"
"No. I'm OK," I said. "Nothing's bothering me."
But I knew my mom was right. I had come up with a plan to deal with this cat thing once and for all. Either it was all my imagination, or they were some sort of evil beings.
While I was getting dressed, I decided on a

plan. Today was library day at school. My English teacher, Mrs. Stacatto, sent the class to the school library every Tuesday to do research or just read books. Most times I looked at sports books. Today, I was going to find out everything I could about cats.

I felt pretty good now that I had a plan. I pulled on my sneakers and took the stairs two at time, hopping down to breakfast.

"No running in the house," said my mom as I came into the kitchen.

"Sorry," I told her. I grabbed a box of cereal and poured a double helping into the bowl. My appetite was back. "Hey, where's the milk?" I asked when I couldn't find any in the refrigerator.

"You tell me," said my mom. She had that look on her face that moms get sometimes when you've done something wrong.

"I don't know," I answered. "Is it a riddle?"

"It certainly is." My mom held up an empty gallon container. "I found this on the floor when I got up this morning. There wasn't a drop left. And it was full yesterday after dinner."

I have never been so happy to get to a library in my life. I ran straight to the computer that listed the books. I typed in "cats", hit the return key, and waited. The screen filled with titles. I hit the print key and raced to the printer, ripping out the page before it had even stopped typing. I didn't bother looking at the names, just the numbers that said where the books were on the shelves.

There were a lot. Not counting magazines and encyclopedias, I'd guess there were fifty. I wanted to read them all. I grabbed armfuls and lugged them over to the nearest table, piling them up. A couple of kids were giving me weird looks, but I didn't care. I hoped one of the books would give me a clue about those mysterious cats.

It was on my third trip back from the shelves that I happened to look down at the title of the top book I was carrying. The old red cover was torn around the edges. It was very plain, and there was nothing special about the book.

Except for the title: *The Cat People*.

Then I read below the title. What I saw made me drop all ten books I was carrying.

It was written by Alan Evans.

Me.

Half of the people in the library came running when they heard the books drop. I wanted to just shrink into a tiny little ant and hide in the corner.

Of course I couldn't. I had to stand there and shrug while the librarian examined me to make sure I was all right. I tried telling her that the books had just slipped out of my hands, but she insisted that there was something wrong with me.

"You look pale." She put her hand to my forehead. "My goodness, I think you have a fever. You must be coming down with something. I'll give you a slip to go see the nurse."

"But I'm fine!" I protested.

"Better safe than sorry," she said, returning to her desk.

"Can I take a book with me to read?"

"Of course you can. Now you go straight to the nurse, do you understand? I'm calling her office right now."

Normally, I would have tried talking her out of it. Just because someone drops some books doesn't mean he's getting the measles. Heck, if it did, kids would be dropping stuff all the time, just to get out of class.

But I wanted to read that Cat People book. And I knew that if I went to the nurse's office, I could read the whole thing in peace while I waited for her to examine me.

The school nurse's office was pretty cool. There were two bunk beds, a cot, and two examining rooms. Plus, in the waiting room there was a real skeleton, with all his bones. The nurse, Miss Sullivan, called him Skinny. Miss Sullivan was a real nice lady, but she always had a lot of work to do. She taught classes and even had to visit some of the other schools in our district. She was almost never in her office.

When someone first went there, one of her aides, usually Mrs. Fleming, would take their temperature and stuff. But even if it was normal, the person had to wait until Miss Sullivan came in.

My temperature was 98.6—exactly right. I saw Mrs. Fleming roll her eyes as she looked at it. "The librarian is a worrywart," she muttered. "All right, Alan," she told me in a louder voice. "I think you're fine, but you'll just have to wait until the boss gets back and gives approval for you to go back to class. I'm afraid it may be an hour."

"That's OK," I said. "I have a book to read."

Did I ever.

I knew I hadn't written the book myself. It wasn't the sort of thing I would do and just forget about. No one would. But it was some coincidence.

The pages were all yellowed and falling apart, and the edges were kind of crinkly. I opened the book carefully and turned to the first page.

"The Legend of the Cat People," it read. "A history of a strange Indian cult, with odd beliefs."

I wasn't sure what the word "cult" meant. Usually I figure out a new word by the other words around it. There wasn't much to go on here. But as I kept on reading, I guessed that it must mean a tribe or group.

The book used a lot of big words and I couldn't understand everything. There was no dictionary in the nurse's office to look stuff up in. I had to read very slowly, rereading some of the sentences two or three times.

The first chapter said that the area where we lived had once been inhabited—that means lived in—by many different Native American tribes. Most of their history was well known. But there was one group that was special. They were very secret. They left very little trace of themselves. Some stone tools and primitive carvings had been unearthed. Otherwise, they had vanished without a trace. Other tribes called them the "Cat People."

The next few chapters were about ruins, and how to figure out what they meant. These chapters were confusing. But I understood chapter five all right. It claimed that the Cat People believed they had a special mission: to fight evil in the world.

It wasn't exactly the same as being a policeman. The Cat People believed there was a supernatural world humans could not see. The battles were fought there. The good and bad powers that fought took the forms of cats.

Not little kitty cats, either. Ferocious man-eaters. Huge, prehistoric giants, with saber-teeth and claws that could pulverize rocks.

One legend said that the Cat People could change back and forth from humans to cats. Another said that humans could not see the cat powers as they truly were. To human eyes, the cats seemed ordinary, even puny.

The author admitted the stories were confusing, even to him.

"One thing the legends make clear," he wrote, "the Cat People must always carry on the fight. If that is true, perhaps they remain among us to this day."

I read that sentence just as Miss Sullivan entered the office. As a matter of fact, I didn't even hear her come in. When she said hello, I just about jumped out of my skin.

"Well, your reflexes are good," she said, smiling. "Let me just double-check your temperature."

It was fine. I went back to class, just in time for math. Mrs. Ferris welcomed me in with a big smile. "Just in time to measure triangles from angles!" she exclaimed, as if we were having a birthday party.

I started reading more of the Cat People book on the bus ride home. Nothing I read told me how to find out if the three cats I'd seen might be the kind in the legends.

Time really does fly when you're busy doing something. It seemed like I had barely sat down when the driver pulled onto my street. I kept looking for something in the book, anything, that might help.

The bus jerked to a stop. Melanie Jagger in the seat across from me hissed that I better hurry. I jumped up and ran for the front.

I was halfway down the bus steps when I saw my three cat friends—or enemies—waiting at the end of my driveway. I grabbed the railing and stopped myself just in the nick of time.

Behind me, the driver was getting huffy.

"Are you getting off, or what?"

"Um, yes," I said. But I didn't move.

"Look buddy, this is your stop. I have a lot of kids waiting."

I could tell that a couple of people in the back of the bus were wondering what was going on. All of a sudden I heard Steve Roberts's voice pipe up.

"Hey, what's with the cats in your yard, Alan? Is that why you're still on the bus? Are you scared of them?"

He had a way of saying "Alan" that fried my stomach. If that old bully was within punching distance, I would have given him a knuckle hero.

With mustard.

But he wasn't. And I didn't want the rest of the kids to think I was a chicken.

I didn't want to be attacked by the cats, though.

Is being a live coward better than being a dead hero? That was one question I didn't want answered.

"I just wanted to make sure I had all my stuff," I told the bus driver. I looked at my backpack as if I weren't positive.

"Do you?"

"I think so," I said. Then I turned to the back where Steve Roberts was sitting. "Who's afraid of cats, Steve?" I said. "The only person I know who's a scaredy-cat is you."

Then I twirled and jumped three steps to the pavement, landing right in front of my feline friends.

Neither the cats nor I moved as the bus roared away. I could hear Steve trying to yell an insult from the window, but it was lost in the exhaust.

I didn't care about him any more. I had a much bigger problem to deal with.

While I stared down the cats, the leopard-colored one leaned across to the gray one and said, "Kid thinks he's pretty brave."

"Let's have him for a snack," purred the brown one. "Probably be as tasty as the lady."

"I heard that, cat," I shouted, pointing at him. "I heard everything. I know who you are. You're evil. You ate Mrs. Johnson, didn't you?"

The cats jumped back. They were stunned and surprised.

That was just the opening I needed. I bolted up the lawn and made it to the front door. I was inside the house before they could even react. I locked it real quick, then ran to make sure the rest of the house was buttoned up tight. When I was sure it was, I went to my sister's room upstairs and snuck over to the half-open window.

There they were, sitting in the driveway, staring at the house. They were talking just loud enough for me to hear. I held my breath and listened.

"Kid understands what we say."

"Impossible. Humans can't understand us."

"I haven't liked him from the start. We should have gotten rid of him when we had the chance."

A car passed by in the road. The noise garbled their words. By the time it had passed, the cats had stopped talking.

Even so, I'd heard plenty. I knew these bad boys were really, truly bad.

Suddenly I realized that my mom was going to come home in a half-hour. And then my sister would arrive. They were both defenseless. Prime targets for the cut-throat kitties.

I grabbed the Cat People book, hoping it would have some secret for dealing with these monsters.

Furiously, I flipped through it. But I couldn't find anything useful. Then I had another idea: what if I could scare them away?

Most cats are afraid of dogs, but there weren't any handy. The Walkers' German shepherd Sweetie Pie was perfect, but there was no way I was going near him. He'd eat me before the cats would. The next closest neighbors who had a dog were the Letteris, and they lived six houses away. Besides, their dog Misha was a black Labrador who was everybody's friend. She couldn't scare a kitten.

Then I had another idea. I didn't need a real dog. I just had to make them think one was nearby.

And there was a good way to do that: ventriloquism.

Normally, the trick takes years to learn—unless you happen to have a pair of walkie-talkies. Which I did.

I raced to my room and grabbed the pair that my uncle Jim had given me last year for my birthday. I knew there wasn't much time. First, I made sure they worked. Then I headed for the back door. My plan was to sneak into Mrs. Johnson's yard and put one in the hedges there.

My hand was on the latch when I realized I would look pretty obvious sneaking along the ground in the bright blue T-shirt I was wearing. I went back upstairs and changed into a dark green shirt and a pair of green pants. Then I found my black bicycle helmet and put it on for good measure. You can't have too much protection sometimes.

I had seen a television show a few weeks before where these commando guys put this black stuff on their faces for camouflage. We didn't have any that I knew of. But I thought I might be able to make a similar effect with some charcoal. I slipped into the garage, grabbed one of the little briquettes, and rubbed my face with it.

While I was there, I took my dad's hatchet from the workbench. No way was I going outside unarmed.

I checked through the window to make sure the cats were still out front. They were. As quietly as possible, I slipped out the back, holding my breath as I crawled into Mrs. Johnson's hedges. Every few feet, I stopped to listen. I couldn't hear anything. Finally, I got close enough to see them. They were still staring at the house. They didn't move. They were waiting patiently for me to come back outside. It was the same way a cat will sit and watch for a bird in a nest. It'll wait all day for the bird to make one false step.

Then bam. Bye-bye birdie.

I slipped the walkie-talkie into the hedges and retreated. Then I went around the back of my house, through my other neighbor Mr. Dix's yard. When I peered around the edge of his house, I saw that they were still in my driveway. Their eyes were fixed on the front of my house.

I put the hatchet down and brought the walkie-talkie close to my mouth. My stomach was doing a wild little dance, but otherwise I felt as calm as a bowl of Jell-O.

In an earthquake.

"Ruff!" I said into the mouthpiece. "Ruff. Ruff."

On paper, it doesn't look very good. But in real life I sounded as tough as Sweetie Pie.

The cats thought so. But instead of scaring them, it made them curious.

And in this case, curiosity did not kill the kitty cat.

"Where's that barking coming from?" I heard one of the cats say.

"I don't see a dog."

"Sounds like he's in the hedges over there."

The gray cat trotted over to investigate. The others followed. I barked as fiercely as I could.

"Must be the puniest dog in the world," said the brown cat. "I'll lick him with one paw tied behind my back."

This wasn't working the way I thought it

would. They were supposed to be scared. Instead, they wanted to find the dog and beat it up.

I growled ferociously, desperate to scare them.

"Hey, look at this," said the gray, tiger-striped cat. "It's some sort of radio thing."

The cats gathered at the edge of the hedges, sniffing at my walkie-talkie.

"I bet that kid is trying to trick us," said the gray cat.

"I already have," I said into the walkie-talkie. I didn't know what else to do. I thought maybe if I sounded like this was all part of my plan, they would be scared enough to run off.

The gray cat pawed at the radio.

"He must be watching us," he said, glancing around. "There he is—look."

The other cats turned. In an instant, their tails shot straight back. The hair on their backs flew up. Gray snarled and took a step in my direction.

As I took a step backward, I caught a glimpse of a car at the end of the road.

My mom was coming home. And she was going to walk right into the middle of the worst cat fight she'd ever seen.

9

For a half-second, I thought—I hoped—that the cats wouldn't see my mom's car, and my mom wouldn't see the cats. There would be three squished cat pancakes in the driveway. The danger would be over.

But just then my sister's school bus pulled up from the other end of the road, flashing its lights. Mom slowed down to stop and wait in the road. She liked to do that to make sure other cars stopped for the bus.

Would the cats attack her with so many people around? Would they jump on my sister as she came off the school bus, even though the driver was there?

I couldn't take a chance. I dropped my walkie-talkie and began running toward them, shouting like a madman. I waved the hatchet in my hand and yelped.

Under the helmet, with my face smeared with black charcoal, I looked like a maniac. Most people would have taken one look at me and run in the other direction.

The cats didn't run away. They kept coming. Their pace was deliberate, faster than a walk but not quite a trot. We were on a collision course.

As I ran I saw Mr. Dix's garden hose on the ground in front of me. That's when I got an idea that saved my life.

At least for a little while.

With a blood-curdling yell—at least I hoped it was—I whipped the ax at the cats, forcing them to change direction for a few seconds. Then I leaped to my right, scooping up the hose in my hands. Luckily, the water was on.

The jet stream caught two of them full in the face, and they yelped as they tumbled backwards. By the time I turned the hose on the third one, he was already in retreat.

Score one for the good guys. I felt happier than I had ever been in my life.

Until I heard Mom's angry voice.

"Alan Daniel Evans! What on earth are you doing with that hose! Why are you dressed like this? Were you playing with your father's hatchet?!?"

My mom was about twenty-hundred-times

madder than I had ever seen her in my life. She grabbed me by the arm and dragged me into the house. I knew I was in for the worst punishment of all time. Even my little sister Dakota Rose was scared. She ran up to her room even though my mom didn't say anything to her.

"I want to hear your explanation," said Mom, standing in the kitchen. If she had calmed down any, it sure didn't show. "What possessed you? What were you thinking? Have you gone stark raving mad?"

The only thing I could think of to do was say I had to show her a book I had gotten from the school library. After she saw it, I added, she could punish me however she wanted.

"That's your answer, a book?" she said, tapping her foot angrily. "Go get it."

I'm sure she thought it was going to be a horror story or something. As I came back down the stairs from my room, I heard her say, "I have a good mind to call up that librarian right now and give her a piece of my mind!"

My mom's face turned white when I handed her the book. She took it from me, and ran her fingers across the cover, as if she were feeling the soft cheeks of a baby's face.

"Where did you get this?" she asked gently.

"In the school library. The person who wrote it has the same name as me."

"He was your great-grandfather," said my mom. She sat down in the chair. "My goodness. Grandpa Al. I didn't know they had a copy of his book."

"Grandpa Al? I was named after him?"

My mother didn't answer. Now it was my turn to ask if she was OK. Mom smiled weakly, then she held out her hands to hug me. I wasn't exactly sure what was wrong, but I knew she needed a hug. So I gave her a good one.

"It's been so long since I thought of him," she said. "Not for eight or nine years at least. Not since I gave his old things to Mrs. Johnson for her files."

"You gave his stuff to Mrs. Johnson?"

"Oh, just some old notes and things that he had given my mother many years ago. Before he disappeared."

"He disappeared?"

My mother nodded. "It wasn't too long after your father and I got married. He was your dad's grandfather."

This was all big news to me. It was shocking that I didn't know. Like someone had landed on Mars without telling the world.

"Why didn't you ever say I was named after someone?" I asked.

"It's a long story," sighed my mother. "Maybe your father should tell you."

"Can't you tell me about him? Grandpa Al?"

"He was your great-grandfather, but everyone called him Grandpa Al. He was a big man, a little gruff, but very kind. He was over ninety when I met him, but he was still very strong. He went for a two-mile walk at least three times a week, without a cane or anything." My mom gritted her teeth, then continued. "One day, he just vanished. Maybe he was senile, and just forgot where he lived. Anyway, the family was never able to find him. It was a terrible tragedy. No one wanted to talk about it. Even now, no one brings it up. I guess your father and I always meant to tell you, but we just never found the right moment."

"He just disappeared?" I asked.

My mom nodded solemnly.

"Mom—the Cat People," I said, pointing to the book.

"Oh, this." She looked at the book and laughed. "Your great-grandpa was an amateur anthropologist. He wrote this book. No one would publish it, so he paid to have it printed himself. He gave all the copies away to libraries."

"An-thro-pologist," I repeated, sounding the word out. "Is that a dinosaur guy?"

"No, honey, that's a paleontologist. An anthropologist looks for the remains of early human civilizations, and tries to figure them out. That's how he came up with this book."

"It's the truth, Mom," I blurted out. "The Cat People exist. In fact, there are three of them outside. I was afraid they were going to attack you and Dakota."

"Alan, look at the title. It says it was a legend. Legends aren't real."

"It is, though. What do you think happened to Mrs. Johnson?"

My mom was still holding me. She shook her head. "Is this why you threw the ax and squirted the hose?"

"I heard the cats talking, Mom. Honest. They were surprised that I could understand them."

"Cats talking? You mean, purring and hissing?"

"No, talking. In English. Like you and me. Their voices are a little high-pitched, but they're easy to understand."

"You're scaring me, Alan. Is this another one of your stories for school?"

"No, it's the truth."

My mom looked at me doubtfully. I'm not sure

67

if she thought I was making it up so I wouldn't get in trouble, or if I was a few eggs short of a dozen.

"What were the things you gave to Mrs. Johnson?" I asked quickly.

"Papers and things. Notes."

"Do you think they're in her room upstairs?" I hoped they were—and that there was more information on the Cat People there.

"Alan, this isn't real. This is legend. A myth. Do you know what that means?"

I knew it was useless to argue with her. Nothing I could say would convince her that I had truly heard the cats talk. So I tried something else.

"I'm supposed to write a report for history class," I told her. This was the truth. We had one due every other week. "I want to write about this book. Even if it's a legend, it would be OK. If Grandpa Al had more notes for this book, I could write a fantastic report. I mean, it would be stupendous."

My mom hesitated.

"You know Mrs. Johnson wouldn't mind," I said. "This is the kind of thing she loves. She's *always* bugging me to use her stuff."

"Yes, but she's not home. And you're still in trouble for playing with the ax."

"I won't do it again," I promised. "And I'll take whatever punishment you decide."

She nodded. "All right. I'll discuss the punishment with your father when he comes home. In the meantime—"

"In the meantime, I have to do my homework. You were going to water Mrs. Johnson's plants today. I can go and do it for you. Besides," I added, "she told me I could use the reports in her attic any time I wanted."

Mom knew I was right, but she still thought about it pretty hard before she agreed. As she took Mrs. Johnson's key out of the kitchen drawer, she described the box that contained Grandpa Al's notes and things. "Don't touch any of her other stuff," my mom warned. "And wash that black junk off your face before you go over there."

69

10

Our showdown with the water hose must have put the cats on notice that I wasn't a pushover. They were nowhere to be seen.

Before I left the house, I stopped in the garage and picked up an old dart gun I'd gotten when I was nine. It had been lying at the bottom of a box of toys and balls and stuff for a year, but it was still as good as new.

It only fired toy darts. But they were better than nothing. I pulled the rubber pieces off. If I hit something with the dart it was going to do some damage.

At least I hoped it would.

My heart almost jumped when I unlocked the door and took my first step into Mrs. Johnson's house. I heard a sound inside somewhere.

Or thought I heard a sound.

Was it my imagination?

Or a cat?

"Mrs. Johnson?" I called.

There was no answer.

"I have the hose!" I shouted, taking another step inside. I hoped that might scare the cats if they were waiting. At the very least, it might get them out of any hiding spots. My finger itched on the trigger of my dart gun.

I must have stood still for a good ten minutes, straining to hear. I bet if there had been an ice cube melting in the kitchen, I would have heard it. But there was nothing. Gingerly, I closed the door behind me.

Knowing about my great-grandfather somehow made me a little braver. I was determined to get to the bottom of this mystery. Carefully, I began edging up the stairs. About halfway up, I heard two quick taps that could only have come from upstairs.

I froze, my back to the wall. Inside my chest, my heart began pounding out a fierce SOS.

In Morse code, that means HELP!!

But there was no one there to hear it.

I couldn't stop now. If I turned back, I would be an easy target on the stairs. The best thing to do was to keep going.

I took another step. There were no more

sounds. Three steps separated me from the top, and whatever danger lurked upstairs.

Another step.

And another quick rap.

It was slightly louder this time. My nightmare was getting impatient.

I eased my finger on the trigger of the dart gun. Would a piece of plastic stop a raging, prehistoric cat monster?

Probably not. But it was all I had.

I'd surprised them with the water before. Maybe I could luck out again this time.

I eased my leg upwards, shifting my weight. Carefully, not daring to breathe, I placed myself on the last step before the top. I was quieter than a stone in an empty forest. The only sound in the house was my pounding heart.

And another gentle rap from the room above.

As I bent down, I caught a glimpse of a shadow at the top of the stair landing. Whatever was waiting lurked just inside the door. I gulped as I saw the hideous outline.

It could only be one thing—one of those cats, its back arched, ready to strike.

But I could get it first. If I dove into the room and fired as it attacked, I'd be sure to hit it.

Was I brave enough?

Then I heard the sound, and it wasn't like I

had a choice anymore. I leaped into action, shouting, screaming, shooting, all at the same time.

Bull's eye.
But it wasn't a cat I hit.
It was a moose head, sitting on the wall right near the door. My dart hit it square in the snout.
That explained the shadow, but not the rapping sound. I jumped to my feet, slamming another dart into the gun. I turned around quickly. At any second I expected to be attacked by three ferocious balls of devilish fur.
Then I saw the blind on the small window moving with the wind. The noise it made was a light tap, exactly what I had heard.
There was nothing up here but me.
I began searching through the boxes for my great-grandpa's. There was enough dust up there to fill a cement mixer. And cobwebs! If I could have somehow gathered them together, they would have made a rope longer than a football field.
After what I had been through, I wasn't going to let a little dust or some dumb spiders slow me down. I knocked the webs away and kept hunting.
When I had been there before, I thought everything was just kind of jumbled together. But now

I realized Mrs. Johnson had actually organized the piles. Everything near the window had to do with stuff that happened in Wappinoe after World War II. The stuff by the door was from the time of the Civil War.

And the Indian stuff was in a small pile against the back wall.

Most of the stuff in the top box marked "Native Americans/Indians" was just drawings. They were based on stories the Wappinoe told about their lives. There were some really cool pictures of what guys did when they hunted and fished. There didn't seem to be any prehistoric cats in them, though.

I sorted through the boxes until I came to the one my mother had described. My mom had gotten the box from work. It had the name of her company on the side.

My heart was beating nearly as fast as when I had climbed up the stairs. I lifted off the cover, and came face to face with my great-grandfather, Alan Evans.

A picture of him, I mean.

He had a beard, and a broad head. He was old, but I couldn't tell how old.

He was also frowning, and looked a little scary.

But I knew that if he had been nice to my mom,

he would be doubly nice to me. Especially since I was named after him.

All of the papers and notes in the box were old and faded. Some of them were typewritten. Most were written out by hand.

I tried to make my eyes into one of those search buttons in a computer program. All I wanted to see were the words "Cat People."

I didn't score any hits until I picked up a small notebook that was tied together with old string. The string was so brittle it disintegrated when I touched it. I opened the cover. The words were penciled in big letters:

"The Cat People—The Untold Story"

I'd found what I had come for.

The pages nearly fell apart in my hands as I leafed through. Yellow and dusty, they looked as if they'd been sitting around for years and years.

But the words jumped right out at me. I nearly fell over when I read them.

"In my book on the Cat People," Grandpa Al wrote on the first page, "I could not write everything I knew about them. I knew no one would believe me. The Cat People still exist. The legend is real."

The rest of the notebook was harder to read. It was all hand-written, and in many places the ink had faded. But I got the main points.

According to my great-grandfather, the Cat People had lived where my subdivision was built. Once, they had been a normal Indian tribe. They didn't even know about the supernatural cat powers. Then one day they found a gravely wounded black puma. They nursed it back to life. It took many months. The whole tribe took turns caring for it.

The puma was really a cat spirit, fighting on the side of good. As a reward, the cat spirit granted the tribe special powers. In each generation, one person would be chosen to help the good side. By putting on a special necklace, the person would gain the supernatural cat powers. It was kind of like being a superhuman hero in a comic book.

The cat spirits could not guarantee that the person would fight for good. In fact, some became bad. But in each generation, a new man put on the necklace to join the fight.

The necklace consisted of a simple string, and a symbol cut in stone. It was called an "amulet." My great-grandfather drew a picture of it. It looked a little like a cat's paw. There were three triangle-shaped wedges at the top where the cat's toes would be. At the bottom, there was another small triangle. There was a hole in the middle, to put the string through.

I nearly fainted when I saw the drawing.

It was the good luck charm on my key ring.

My heart was pounding as I brought the notebook back to my house. I was so excited I didn't consider that the cats might be waiting to ambush me.

Lucky for me they weren't.

Mom was sitting at the kitchen table waiting when I came in. She had a worried look on her face.

"Look what I found, Mom. Great-Grandpa wrote a whole other book on the Cat People. It's a notebook."

"Alan, come sit here a minute," she said.

"What's wrong, Mom?"

"You know the difference between real and make-believe, don't you?"

"Of course. Don't you?"

Mom's face looked like she had just drunk some grapefruit juice.

"These things, they're all make-believe," she said.

"Grandpa Al thought they were real," I said.

"I think you should talk to your dad when he comes home, OK?"

"Sure."

"Here, come here and give me a hug."

I gave her a big one, then I headed upstairs to read more of the book. I also wanted to look for a piece of string, so I could hang the amulet around my neck, like it said in the book. There was an old kite in my closet. The string was tangled but I managed to cut off a piece long enough. I took the stone amulet and worked it off the key chain.

The stone had always brought me a lot of luck. I had rubbed it right before my Little League team won its first baseball game. I had it in my pocket when I scored a hundred on my first science test. There were a ton of other things. But I have to admit, until then, I wasn't positive it really worked. My dad was an engineer. Once I told him about keeping the good luck charm with me when my Little League team played. He called it a coincidence that we won. The charm didn't have anything to do with it, he said. Good stuff and bad stuff happens, and you just deal with it.

Maybe he was right. But the moment I put the necklace with the stone around my neck, I felt something I had never felt before. My chest tingled inside, as if something were tickling my lungs. The muscles in my arms and legs started to stretch on their own. And my eyes—it was like all of a sudden I could see about ten times better.

Had I become a supernatural being?

I ran directly to the mirror in the bathroom.

I was still a normal, ordinary boy.

Not ordinary, exactly. I noticed that the whites of my eyes seemed to glow. But otherwise, I looked exactly the same. My clothes still fit. I didn't have any whiskers or anything growing out of my nose. I felt just like I did before, only stronger, with better eyesight.

I went back into my room and picked up Grandpa Al's notebook. I learned two things that I thought were more important than anything else. One was that you could tell the good from the bad cats by the color of their eyes. Red was evil, white was good.

I couldn't remember what color my three friends' eyes had been. It was pretty easy to guess, though.

The other thing I read in the notebook was scarier.

"The human follower of the cat spirits must always be on his guard," Great-Grandpa wrote, "for the evil ones will seek to recruit him into their foul coven. Once your eyes become red, you may never go back. You will be an evil cat until death, or the end of time."

A shudder ran through my spine when I read that. Then something grabbed me on the shoulder. It felt like a claw.

"Hey, Alan, what's up?"
I jerked around and saw my dad smiling behind me.

"I didn't mean to scare you," he added, letting go of my shoulder. "What are you reading?"

"I found this book that Grandpa Al wrote."

"Your mom told me. What was that business about the hatchet?"

I gulped. For a second I thought of explaining everything. Then I decided it was smarter to wait until I was sure he would believe me, or until I had proof to convince him I was telling the truth.

"I guess I got a little scared."

"Of cats?"

"I read Grandpa Al's book in the library, Dad."

My father nodded. He got a real serious look on his face all of a sudden, then sat on the edge of the bed. It didn't take a fortune-teller to figure out what he was going to talk about.

"Son, I think I should tell you a thing or two about your great-grandfather," said my dad. He sighed so deeply I thought the walls were going to shake. "He was my grandfather. I loved him a lot. Grandpa Al was a brilliant man when he was younger. Some say he was a genius. He taught history at a college. Then he decided to study anthropology. Do you know what that is?"

"Mom told me."

Dad nodded, but explained it anyway. "Anthropology is the science of human beings," he said. His voice got slow, like it always does when he's trying to explain stuff. "Where they came from, how they lived in the past."

"It's like history, right?"

"Well, like history, yes," agreed my dad. "Only further back. And there are guesses involved. There's less evidence to go on. An anthropologist might study the ruins of an ancient city. Like Egypt, for example. He or she might look at the pyramids, and figure out who the people were who built them."

"Or he could look at Native Americans," I suggested.

"Yes, he would look at Native Americans," agreed my dad.

"That's what Grandpa Al did. He discovered the Cat People."

I knew that was a mistake as soon as I said it.

"Alan, your great-grandfather, well, at the end, he was a bit, I don't know how to put it—"

"You think he was nuts, dad?"

"A little. He really believed the legends were true."

"I know he did." I touched the amulet around my neck.

"You're wearing your good luck charm?" my dad asked.

I nodded. I almost told him that it would give me special powers. Then I thought, if he thinks

Grandpa Al was crazy, what would he think about me?

"You know, your great-grandfather found that in a field not far from here," my dad told me. "When the shopping center was being built. I still remember the day he gave it to me."

"Really?"

"Yes," said my father sadly. "It was the last day I saw him."

"Where did he go?"

"Well, no one knows. I guess you're old enough to understand. The police told us he must have wandered off somewhere and died. We were all very sad. It was horrible. He must have been alone and without his family."

I nodded, even though I suspected something else had happened. Something much different.

"I'm sorry we never told you," added my dad. "It was very sad for us all. He disappeared right after you were born."

"I understand."

My father got up off the bed. "Don't play with the hatchet any more. It's not a toy."

"I know. I'm sorry."

Trying to smile, my dad pointed at the stone. "Still bringing you good luck?"

"All the time."

"You know, he thought it had special powers."

83

"Maybe it does," I said. "Who knows?"

For just a second, my dad frowned. I thought he was going to give me another lecture. But then he surprised me.

"Maybe it does," he said. "Who knows how these things work?"

We went down to dinner. I was hungrier than anything. We were having spaghetti. I had three helpings. That was a world record for me.

Nothing much happened the rest of the night. My sister tried to start a dumb fight, but I ignored her. There were more important battles brewing.

When I got ready for bed, I kept the stone amulet around my neck. I slipped under the covers. I could see really well in the room, even though the lights were off. It was awesome.

I got tired real fast. As soon as my head touched the pillow, I started to yawn. Two yawns, and my eyes were closing. I tried to keep them open, checking out the room in the dark and stuff. But in less than three seconds, I was asleep.

The next thing I knew, I felt something breathe right into my face. Still groggy, I opened my eyes and found myself eyeball to eyeball with a gray saber-toothed tiger.

12

I was so scared my heart nearly flew out my rib cage. But the tiger didn't eat me or anything. Not at all. He jumped back off the bed. I noticed the window behind him was wide open.

I knew I had locked it down good and tight before I went to bed.

I wasn't dreaming, either—I pinched myself just to make sure.

"So, you're one of us, aren't you?" said the tiger, prowling back and forth across the room from me. "It will seem scary at first," he added. "But once you get the hang of it, you'll see there's nothing better. We can do whatever, wherever, whenever we want. Your powers are far beyond anything you've ever dreamed."

It sure sounded cool. But I was still scared. I mean, there was a big, saber-toothed tiger, with gray fur and dark stripes, standing a few feet away from me. Talking.

"Come on," he said. "Let me show you what the universe really looks like."

"B-But I'm still a k-kid," I stuttered. I touched the amulet under my pajama top, hoping it would make me feel less scared.

He laughed. "Oh, I forgot. You haven't learned how to transform yourself yet. It's very easy. All you have to do is believe." The tiger took a step toward me. "Here, let me help you."

"No!" shouted a deep voice that seemed to come from outside of the house.

I looked up at the window. A huge black cat flew inside with a mighty leap. Its thick fur glistened in the night. Two long, gleaming white tusks hung from its mouth. They were as sharp as swords. The cat looked like a giant, powerful black puma. It growled angrily at the other cat.

"Leave the boy alone," it demanded. The puma's voice sounded deeper than the others had. It was more like a person's.

"Make me," snarled the gray tiger.

"With pleasure," snapped the puma.

The cats fell together in a ferocious tumble. They snarled and screamed as they crashed around the room. The noise was louder than a hurricane. Finally, the tiger broke free. He quickly turned and looked at me.

"Are you coming?" he asked.

His eyes glowed fiery red in the darkness. They made me shudder. I remembered my grandfather's warning. Once you're bad, you can never go back.

"No!" I said.

He growled. "I shall return."

The puma swiped at the tiger's backside with his paw. The tiger groaned, then leapt through the window. He was gone.

"You're safe for now," said the puma, when he had caught his breath. "But he'll be back. I'm sure of it."

The big cat's eyes glowed white. That was a relief.

"My parents, they're sure to be in here any second," I said. "The noise from your fight must have woken them up."

"Be at ease," said the puma. "The fight did not take place in the human world. They heard nothing of it. Look at your furniture. Is it broken?"

I looked at the furniture and realized he was right. Nothing had been harmed. The way those two had been going at it, there should have been nothing left but sawdust.

"Nothing we do directly affects the human

world," said the puma. He stood close to me as he spoke. For some reason, I wasn't afraid of him at all. "Man-made objects, like your furniture, are not harmed. Things in the natural world, like trees and rocks, are different. They can be destroyed, and often are.

"My name is Takar," he added. "My friends call me Tak. I hope you'll be one of them."

"Thank you, Tak," I said. "My name is Alan."

"A good human name," said the cat. "But you will need something better when you join us."

"What if I don't want to join you?"

The cat laughed. This was a new sound to me, but then again, everything was pretty new. It sounded a little like bells ringing. "It is your choice. But no human has ever resisted. Not even your great-grandfather."

"Grandpa Al?"

"We call him Alpha. He has taken the shape of the White Lion. Perhaps you will meet him someday."

"I'd like that," I said.

"Come then, you can take your first adventure."

"How?"

"The power to transform yourself is within you. Envision the form you wish to take, and you will become it."

"That's it?"

"That's it. Repeat these words. They will help you. *'Let me fight evil in the world! Make me a cat spirit!'*"

It sounded too wild to be true. There was only one way to find out. I closed my eyes, and pretended I was a saber-toothed tiger.

With yellow-and-brown fur, and a little bigger than the one the puma had chased out of the room. Just in case.

"Let me fight evil in the world!" I said. "Make me a cat spirit."

Nothing happened for a second. In fact, nothing happened at all. I opened my eyes and looked around the room.

"I think you're pulling my leg," I told the cat.

"Which one? You have four."

I looked down quickly, expecting it was a "made-you-look" joke.

But it wasn't. I did have four legs. And they were huge, and covered with striped yellow and brown fur. I opened my mouth in awe.

That's when I felt how heavy my teeth were.

"You can't see your teeth unless you look in a mirror," Tak told me. He laughed again. "There's a limit even to our powers."

Hopping out of bed felt weirder than weird. I thought I was using just two feet. You know, like a normal kid. But as I moved, I landed on all fours. Boy, did it take some getting used to. It was almost like learning to walk all over again. At least there was no way to fall on my backside.

Finally, I reached the mirror. I did have tusks. They were white and gleamed, even in the dark. Man, did they look sharp. I probably could have split a hair with them.

"Run around the room a little," suggested Tak. "Get used to how it feels to be a saber-toothed tiger."

I took a few turns in the room. My room wasn't exactly the biggest room in the house, so I couldn't go very fast or very far. Then I tried to jump over the bed. It was a great jump—until I landed. My head crashed into the wall.

"Are you all right?" Tak asked. He was standing over me.

"I didn't realize I could jump so far," I said.

"You'll be amazed at your abilities," he told me. "Maybe we better go outside."

"But what about my parents?"

"They won't know you're gone. You can come back and change into a normal kid again."

"I can?"

"As long as you don't eat any meat while you're a cat, you can change back and forth. In fact, until you get much older, it would be better for you to stay human as much as possible."

"How come?"

"How many saber-toothed tigers have you seen in math class?" asked Tak sarcastically. "The more you learn as a human, the smarter you will be as a cat spirit. And we need smart cats to fight the Bads."

"The Bads?"

"That's what we call the evil ones. The good cats like us are called the Brave. Don't let the Bads trick you. Once you join them, you can never go back."

"In the human world, someone who's bad can repent," I said.

"Good for humans. It doesn't work that way for us," said Tak. "Come on now, let's play before your stomach starts growling."

And with that, he leapt through the window.

I went to it and peered out. My bedroom is on the second floor. It sure looked like a long way down.

But I couldn't chicken out now. I took a deep breath, closed my eyes, and dove forward into a strange new world.

13

I felt a lot of different things in that second as I jumped out the window. Most of them I can't put into words.

It's real easy to say what the biggest thing was, though—fear.

I certainly wasn't used to being a cat yet. It felt like I was belly-flopping into a pool, with my hands and legs spread. Except that wasn't warm, blue water waiting for me below. It was cold, hard ground.

The wind made a whooshing sound around me. The air poked at me with thousands of pins, pricking every part of my body. I could see really well, but that wasn't a good thing—the ground came up real quick.

Then my arms and legs flicked into position below the rest of my body. Maybe this is how a jet would feel putting down landing gear—that is, if a jet could feel.

I hit the ground, not with a slam and a bash, but with a gentle nudge. It was almost as if a parachute had opened from my back.

My new pal, the saber-toothed puma, was waiting on the lawn for me.

"You passed your first test," said Tak. "Landing like a cat. It's part of your instincts."

"Will I always land on my feet?"

"In theory," said Tak. "But let's not push it. You still have a lot to learn. Come. Let's take a stroll. Remember—don't eat anything."

Tak jogged toward the street. I started behind him. I nearly tripped over my front feet with my first step. I did trip over them on my second, landing in a tumble. When I looked up, I saw a striped brown-and-yellow snake right in front of me.

I was scared, but I knew that a tiger shouldn't be afraid of anything. So I growled, hoping it would back away.

It didn't move. That made me a little angry. Who did that stupid snake think he was, tangling with a tiger?

I took a swipe at it, and struck it across the face. At the same instant, I felt a sharp pain in my back. Shrieking, I jumped to my feet. Spinning quickly, I hissed at whatever had attacked me. But it had vanished.

"Trying to catch your tail?" asked Tak. He was holding back a laugh.

"A snake just attacked me," I said. "It hurt."

"Oh, really?" he grinned. "What color was the snake?"

"Brown and yellow."

"Tiger colors?"

"Well, maybe."

Tak started laughing out loud.

"It's not funny," I protested. "It hurts!"

"Just be thankful you didn't bite it," he said. "Come on. Let's get going."

"I'm having trouble walking," I said, almost falling again.

Tak sighed. "Don't think about it, just do it." He turned abruptly and trotted across the road.

I had no choice but to follow. His advice was right on the mark. There was something inside me that seemed to know how to be a cat. All I had to do was let it act naturally, and I would be OK. It was only when I really thought about something that I ran into trouble.

Like after I ran across the street and tried to stop. Smash, tumble, crash—I knocked over a whole row of garbage cans in my neighbor Mr. Walker's yard.

A light snapped on in one of the rooms. "Hey,

what's going on out there?!?" yelled Mr. Walker, yanking open the window above.

I looked up and snarled. I could see Mr. Walker's face clearly—it was round and red and angry. His big mustache twitched. "I'm trying to sleep in here. What's out there? Who is it? Is that a cat? I'll sic my dog on you, I will!"

"Come on," growled Tak beside me, "let's scoot before he throws something. He sees us as cats, not as Goods."

I was a little scared, so I didn't think about how to move as we ran behind the house. With one step, Tak cleared the picket fence.

And so did I!

Right into the yard where Sweetie Pie was sleeping.

The dog's eyes opened with a start.

"Does he think we're puny little cats?" I asked Tak.

"Growl and find out," he suggested.

So I did. It wasn't anything special. Just an ordinary, I'm-going-to-grind-you-to-a-pulp growl.

The German shepherd's eyes opened wide for a second. He took one step toward me. Then he dove into his little dog house, yelping like he'd just seen a ghost.

Or a saber-toothed tiger.

Boy, did that make me feel good. That stupid dog had bothered me for years.

"Other animals will see you as you are, if you desire it," explained Tak. "Or you can make them think you're a harmless tabby. It's up to you. As soon as you thought of yourself as a tiger, he saw it and fled."

I wanted to have some more fun with the dumb dog, but Tak said we had better things to do. He ran on through the backyard, cutting into another neighbor's property. I followed. I knew where I was, but everything seemed different. It was like looking at the world from a new angle. No night had seemed this bright. Plus, I had all sorts of new smells coming into my nose. I could smell the chlorine in Mr. Paxton's pool real strong, and some perfumey thing from Ms. Clearwater's garden. And the garbage—wow, was it strong!

Suddenly, a smell entered my cat-snout that was really something else. It was a bit like chicken legs on a barbecue. I had to stop and take a deep, deep whiff of the air. I could almost taste it. My stomach started rumbling, and I knew I had to try whatever it was.

Without even knowing what I was doing, I took a step in the direction of the smell. Then another and another and another.

Somewhere along the way, I realized it wasn't a barbecued chicken. It was too late for anyone to be grilling. But whatever it was, it smelled great. I ran and ran.

Finally, I saw what it was—a rabbit. It was sleeping in a pen in Janice Clearwater's yard. The fence surrounding the pen was about three feet high. I leaped it in a flash. I had the rabbit pinned beneath my right paw before it even woke up.

I had never felt so hungry in my life. The saliva drooled from my mouth as I opened my jaws, ready to gobble the bunny up.

Stunned, the rabbit blinked open its bright pink eyes. A tear started to form in one of them. It saw me as a tiger and I guess it knew it was a goner.

The tear made me stop for just a second. Then I heard Tak come up behind me.

"Don't eat it!" he screamed. "You won't be able to change back."

Letting go of that rabbit was the hardest thing I ever did. The poor pet scurried behind its little box. I jumped back over the fence before I could change my mind.

Tak had already started trotting away. I hustled to keep up with him. He leaped over the small stone wall at the back of the yard, then went through another yard. I didn't know exactly where we were until we came around the side of a garage. The elementary school was dead ahead.

"Look out for cars," Tak warned as he bolted across the road.

I glanced in both directions—there was nothing in sight—then followed. He jogged up toward the front of the building, checking around. Heading toward the back, he stopped suddenly.

That's when I smelled it. The best way to describe what filled my nostrils is with one word: YUK.

My stomach nearly turned with the stench.

"Looks like you're going to get your first lesson in fighting," said Tak, turning to me. "I was hoping to wait for a while, but your friend wants to be a pest."

"My friend?"

"The striped gray tiger who tried to recruit you before. His name is Stinkular. We call him Stinky. I guess you can tell why."

"I sure can."

"Flail your head around when you first see him. That will let him know that you mean business. If he runs at you, stand your ground."

"Will he attack me?"

"He may. If so, let your instincts take over.

Don't try to fight like a human would. Fight like a cat."

Before I could ask another question, Tak leapt forward. All I could do was follow.

Fight like a cat? Let my instincts take over?

The advice wasn't exactly helpful. Luckily for me I didn't have too much time to think about it. I had to run pretty fast to keep up with Tak. Before I knew it, we were trotting toward the baseball field.

And there was Stinky. The smell got worse as we got closer.

I could hear Tak growling at him as we ran.

"What are you doing here, evil one? You know this ground is sacred to the Cat People. Many Braves are buried here."

"The Cat People are my tribe, too," said Stinky. "I have as much right as you do to be here. Call yourself Brave if you want. You are still a weakling."

"Scat," growled Tak, pulling up a few yards from the evil cat. "Leave."

"So, you've joined the goodie-goods," Stinky snarled at me. "How does it feel?"

"It feels very good," I said. I sure hoped I sounded brave.

"You're still young. You will be very valuable

to us," said Stinky. "Some day, you could be our leader."

He took a step toward me. Tak immediately darted in his way. But ol' Stinky was ready for that—he faked to the left and dodged right, and in a flash two very sharp saber-teeth were headed straight for me.

I held my ground as best I could. I told myself not to be scared.

Stinky stopped a few inches from my face. I could feel his putrid breath on my chest. Tak turned around and watched. He was right behind him.

"Leave me alone," I said. I could feel my tail getting stiff behind me. My claws felt hard and sharp in my paws.

"You have courage," snarled Stinky. "Must run in the family. But you won't last."

That's when he jumped me.

If there had been any warning, I probably would have died right there. Stinky threw his fangs at my throat. Their knife-like points could have ripped a huge hole in my neck. That would have been the end.

But because I didn't have a warning, I didn't have time to think and my cat instincts took over. I ducked to the side, pulling my whole body to the ground. In the next second, I leapt forward.

My teeth caught the big bad cat right in the belly. Blood gushed from an oozing gash.

Give Stinky credit. That gore in his belly must have hurt worse than anything he'd ever known. Still, he fought on. Rolling over, he flailed with his claws. He tried to bite me, but I quickly stabbed his stomach again.

We rolled around in the dirt for a few seconds more, snarling and snapping at each other. Then Tak leapt onto his back. Stinky howled with pain. He squirmed desperately. Finally, he managed to escape, but just barely.

"Let him go," said Tak as I started to follow. "It will take several hours for his wounds to heal."

"That's all?" I was astonished.

"Remember, the cat spirits are supernatural. Our healing powers are tremendous. The Bads are even more difficult to kill than we are. But we are all mortal. If you die while you are in cat form, you die as a human. That's why you must always be very careful. You understand?"

I nodded.

Tak licked my wounds. Instantly, they healed. "You'll soon be out of energy," he told me. "Come, you've had a busy night. It's time for you to go home and rest."

My head felt a little shaky. I followed Tak through backyards, over fences, and around swimming pools. Finally, I found myself back in front of my house.

"I have to leave you now. I have many other duties to perform. And you must go and rest. I'll meet you here again tomorrow night," he told me. "Try to stay out of trouble until then."

Tak started to bound away.

"Wait!" I cried. "I'm still a saber-toothed tiger! What will my parents say?"

But Tak had already bolted over the hedges at the back of our yard. There was no way I could catch him now.

I had never felt so alone in my life. And I was standing on my own front lawn! I didn't know exactly what to do. I was real hungry, but I knew I couldn't eat anything. I also couldn't stay out here. Stinky and his friends might come back. But what would mom or dad think if they found a saber-toothed tiger in my room?

Yell, scream, and call the police, I guessed.

Then I remembered that they would see me as a harmless kitty cat. Still, that was almost as bad. Mom was allergic to cats. She would hand me over to the animal shelter. Or at least put me in the garage.

I couldn't stay here, though. I had come through my first fight all right, but that was just luck. If I had been thinking about what to do, I never could have done it. I would have been cat food. The best thing to do was go in my room and lock the window. Maybe I could somehow pretend I was sick when Mom came to wake me. Then I could stay in bed all day until Tak came back.

I took a step backward on the lawn. My window was still open. I figured one good leap and I would be inside.

I figured wrong. Bam! With a crash I hit the side of the house. Only by instinct did I put out my paws and grab on to the siding.

After I caught my breath, I pulled myself up and climbed inside. I pushed down the window behind me. But my paws were too clumsy to lock it.

My adventure had made me dead tired. I took a step toward my bed. I was so pooped I tripped over my front foreleg and went plop on the little rug near the dresser. I looked up, then realized this was as good a place to sleep as any. Before I could think anything else, I was snoozing.

14

"Alan! What are you doing sleeping on the floor?"

I woke with a start, twisting over so I could jump to my four feet.

Except that there were only two of them. I shot up, only to fall forward on my face. Luckily for me, the bed was right there. Still, I looked pretty dumb as my head rebounded off the mattress.

"Alan? Are you OK?" My mom helped me up. "Are you all right?"

I nodded yes. I was, too. Somehow, I was back in human form, dressed in my pajamas.

"What happened to your face?" my mother asked.

I felt for my teeth right away. The only thing I could think of was that my saber-teeth were still there.

But that wasn't it.

"You slept on the rug so long, it left an imprint," said my mom. She inspected my face. "Honestly, Alan, lately you do the strangest things."

I didn't dare tell her how right she was.

The rest of that morning and a lot of the school day went by in a blur. I ate three helpings of cereal for breakfast, and packed an extra sandwich for lunch. Mom said she was happy to see that I had my appetite back.

I didn't pay much attention in most of my classes. When I got to English, I asked my teacher if I could go to the library. I wanted to see if there were any books about Indians that might tell me more about the Cat People. But she said no because we were watching a movie.

I didn't watch much of the movie. I saw a castle and a car at the beginning. That was about it. Instead of paying attention, I thought of the questions I wanted to answer. I wrote them down in my notebook as the movie played.

Would I only change back to being a kid when I slept?
How long could I stay a cat without eating?
Would I always become the same sort of cat?
What if one of the bad cats managed to gore

me while I was fighting it? Would the gore hurt me as a human?

But my biggest question was this:

Tak had said my great-grandpa was one of them. How could I meet him?

I kept writing questions as the movie played. Suddenly, I realized that the movie was over. The lights were on. I looked up and realized that the teacher was talking. Her face was a little on the red side. She was definitely mad about something.

"I could tell that most of you weren't paying attention during this film," said Mrs. Stacatto. "I saw a lot of people talking and even sleeping. But I know at least one student was. He took very copious notes."

Everybody scratched their head, trying to figure out what "copious" meant. It turned out it's a fancy way of saying "a lot."

Mrs. Stacatto started calling on kids, asking them to summarize the movie. There were a lot of stutters and stuff. No one in the class had paid attention.

I sunk lower and lower in my chair. Then I heard my name called.

"Mr. Evans can give us a summary, I'm sure," said the teacher. She looked at me as proudly as Mom did when I brought home an A. Then she added, "He took notes."

Boy, talk about your heart sinking to your feet. I think my tongue tied itself into a triple granny knot. Here was the teacher, looking at me like I was Mr. Teacher's Pet.

And every kid was staring at me with cat eyes. They all hated me.

Not that I could blame them. But I sure did wish I could come up with something to say other than "a car and a castle."

"That was it? Read something from your notes."

"I'd rather not," I said.

Everybody else in class started snickering. Luckily for me, the bell rang.

I was about to get on the bus to go home when an announcement over the loudspeaker reminded me that there was an important after-school meeting today.

"Everyone interested in trying out for next year's football team, report to Room 103," it said.

"Late buses will be provided after the end of the meeting."

I stopped in my tracks. I had been planning on going to that meeting for at least a couple of weeks. But I'd forgotten all about it.

To be honest, I wasn't sure I should bother. I mean, with all this cat stuff to do, there might not be time for football next year.

But Tak had told me I would have to stay in school to learn more. And if I had to do that, then I might just as well play football. Besides, maybe I could use my new powers. A saber-toothed tiger as linebacker was sure to end up being an all-county star.

The meeting turned out to be pretty interesting. The high school freshman coach, Mr. Fisco, stopped by and gave everyone a big pep talk. Then he handed out papers with some exercises to do over the summer. He also passed out a sheet with healthy stuff to eat. I figured both would help me, even if I didn't play football.

Afterwards, we went out to one of the fields behind the school and tossed a football around. Ordinarily, that's the kind of thing I like. But I kept daydreaming about being a saber-toothed tiger. I didn't pay attention, and missed a couple of easy catches.

Finally, the bell rang and we all headed for the late bus. I figured that there would be just enough time to finish my homework before dinner. Then after dinner, I would go upstairs to my room and wait for Tak to arrive.

I planned on eating three helpings of supper. I hoped Mom had cooked something extra special. Even if she cooked spinach casserole, I planned on eating until my belly popped. That way, I'd have more energy when I turned into a cat.

On the bus home, I held the stone amulet in my hand. I looked at it and thought about its power. I also thought about my encounter with Stinky the night before. I was excited that I could help fight evil. It was like being in a movie, only it was happening to me in real life.

I knew I had a lot to learn. I guessed that Grandpa Al had studied for years before he joined the cat spirits. He was a leader now. I planned to follow in his footsteps.

Make that his *paw* prints.

I also planned on having a lot of fun being a saber-toothed tiger. The first thing I hoped to do tonight was scare Mr. Walker's dog Sweetie Pie again.

By the time the bus turned the corner onto my street, my heart was racing. I was so excited that I jumped off the last three steps of the bus onto the pavement in front of my house.

That's when I saw my sister, Dakota Rose, trapped by Stinky and his two friends.

15

Stinky and his two pals were circling Dakota on the driveway. I knew that to her eyes, they were just cats. Even so, they looked scary. They had their fur up and were hissing. The strange way they were acting made her afraid. She was almost crying.

I could see them as they truly were—big, mean, ugly, evil beasts. Stinky, the gray tiger, rolled his saber-toothed jaw back and forth. Behind him, a saber-toothed leopard slashed the air with his extended claws. The brown cat, a saber-toothed lynx, drooled with anticipation.

"Dakota, go inside!" I yelled.

"These cats won't let me," she whimpered. She took a step to the left. So did the cats.

"Mom!" I yelled.

"She can't hear you," sneered Stinky, in his familiar high-pitched whine. Even though I was still in human form, his foul odor stung my nose.

"Mom! Call the police!" I yelled.

"By the time they get here," snarled the lynx, "your sister will be catnip. Just like your neighbor."

"Mmmmm," leered the leopard. "I can taste this one already."

Stinky took a step toward her. I dropped my backpack and books. "Leave her alone!" I shouted. "Or I'll beat you up like I did last night."

"You won't be so brave without Tak to help you this time," said Stinky. The sun gleamed off the knife-points of his teeth. "Besides, there's three of us, and only one of you."

"Run, Dakota!" I shouted, grabbing the amulet around my neck. In the same breath, I whispered, "Let me fight evil in the world! Make me a cat spirit!"

A million things seemed to happen at once. My sister ran for the door. Stinky leapt after her. And I jumped on Stinky, flailing my fists.

Which had become the knife-like claws of a saber-toothed tiger.

The fight was ferocious. Dakota managed to yank open the door as I dug my claws into Stinky's side. He yelped in pain. The lynx ran after my sister. I pushed Stinky aside and caught the little devil in two bounds. I scooped my tusks under him and gave a mighty heave. He flew over my shoulder, as light as a kitten.

Dakota escaped inside. I would have followed her, but just then I felt a sharp pain in my leg. I was dragged backward from the door.

The leopard had his mouth around my ankle. I screamed and snarled, then tried to bat him off with my foreleg. It didn't work. I felt myself being hauled back onto the driveway.

Stinky jumped on top of me. I rolled desperately around. Somewhere along the way, the lynx joined in, too. We were one big cat pile, tumbling, scratching, snarling, and slashing at each other. All I could see was fur and it was flying.

Somehow, I managed to work free. I started to run. I didn't pay any attention to where I was going. I just ran. I knew I was no match for all three cats together. I hoped I could find a place to hide.

Of course, the others didn't want me to escape. They ran after me like police chasing a bank robber. I'm not exactly sure which yards or even streets I went down. I just ran and jumped. I squeezed through fences, and ran, ran, ran for my life.

Finally, I reached the elementary school field. I was exhausted. I dropped down to my stomach, panting.

The others were nowhere to be seen. I thought I had escaped.

But I was wrong. They were just catching their breath out of sight. In half a minute, they appeared, each one coming from a different direction. They walked toward me slowly.

I rose to my feet. I knew I didn't have enough energy to run away. My only hope was to stand and fight.

"Here he is, the brave warrior," sneered the lynx.

"I'll do the talking," snapped Stinky, the gray tiger. "Watch out that he doesn't try to escape."

"I'll fight you here," I said as bravely as I could. I rocked my weary shoulders back and forth, getting ready for their attack.

"Don't be in such a hurry to be whipped," said Stinky. His voice sounded almost pleasant. "What do you call yourself, anyway?"

"My name is Alan Evans," I said.

"That's your human name," said the gray tiger. "What is your cat name?"

"I don't have one yet."

"Modred's a nice name," suggested the leopard.

I could tell they were up to something. They were trying to pretend they were my friends.

"Nah. He looks like a Luther to me," said the gray tiger. They had me surrounded. I looked at each one in turn. I hoped that would keep them away.

"I don't want any of your names," I said. "I'll wait to see what Tak suggests."

The gray tiger laughed. "Tak is a sissy. You shouldn't take advice from him."

"He's a goodie-good," sneered the leopard.

"He's my friend."

"You should be *our* friend," said the gray tiger. "We can show you all sorts of things. Much better than Tak."

"We'll take you hunting," said the leopard. "We'll show you how to beat up dogs, and climb trees."

"I can do those things already," I said.

"But you can't fly," said Stinky. And all of a sudden he leapt into the air.

I watched as he floated there. It was truly amazing.

"Tak didn't tell you that we could fly, did he?" demanded Stinky. "He didn't tell you half of our powers. Goods can't fly. They can't do half the cool stuff we can do."

"Join us," said the leopard. He nudged closer to me. "You won't have to go to school anymore. We'll teach you to fly and you can go anywhere in the world."

114

"We'll pop on down to Disney World tonight, if you like," suggested the lynx.

"Disney World?" I asked. I'm ashamed to admit it, but they had found my weakness. I actually considered joining them for half a second.

"Of course," said Stinky. He shot upward, then to the right. Then he did a loop-de-loop, exactly like an airplane. Finally, he floated down to earth in front of me. "We can go right now, if you like. We'll wait until the park closes, then we'll start up all the rides, just for you."

"You're trying to trick me," I said.

"No, we're not. Everything we've said is true."

"But you want me to be evil, just like you."

"Is that such a bad thing?" asked the leopard.

"Yes, if you scare little girls like my sister. Or eat people like my neighbor."

"Aw, that's just what cats do," said Stinky. His voice was as smooth as silk. "It's our nature. Instincts. You have them, too. Go on. Admit it."

"No!" I screamed, lunging at him. "I'm not evil! I'm good!"

My attack surprised the gray tiger. I dug my fangs into his neck before he could retreat. The others jumped on me, trying to pull me away. I wouldn't let go. Finally, the lynx managed to hurt me in the side, and I had to retreat. Stinky slumped onto the ground. He was barely breathing.

The gray tiger had been the most ferocious of the bunch. But the lynx and the leopard were still tough customers. They bared their teeth as they stalked back and forth, looking for an opening to attack. I waved my two pointy sabers in their direction. My heart was pounding faster than a jet engine at takeoff. The fight with Stinky had been short, but it had taken a lot out of me.

I prayed someone would come along and scare the other cats away. They were mad now that their leader was lying dying on the ground. They were out for blood.

My blood.

Suddenly, the lynx dove at me. I ducked his saber-toothed mouth. Then I spun back. Just as I suspected, the leopard was attacking. We rolled together in a furious tumble. Neither one of us could get an advantage. He clawed at my face. I bit one of his paws. I tried to stick my tusk in his side. He yanked it away with his foot.

I felt a sharp pain in my tail. I jerked my head up. By accident, I knocked my skull right into the leopard's. He fell back, woozy. I rolled around just in time to get whacked by the lynx's outstretched claws. He raked them across my shoulder. Blood streamed out like anti-freeze from a busted car radiator. I snapped my jaws together on his leg so hard I almost bit it off. He whimpered and ran away. He was a coward at heart.

Meanwhile, the leopard had grabbed the gray tiger by the scruff of the neck. He began dragging him off to safety. They'd all had enough fight for one day. I took a step toward them, but then collapsed, exhausted, and critically wounded.

6

I have no idea how long I lay in the grass. Blood seeped from at least a dozen wounds. My head felt like it had been hit with a baseball bat. My legs felt worse. One of my saber teeth had been chipped. My tail had been bitten. Even my fur hurt.

Above everything else, I was starving. I had used a tremendous amount of energy. My stomach felt like a crumbled-up can of soda on a hot summer's day.

I hoped someone—anyone—would come along and take me to a hospital or something. I knew that a human would see me as just another cat. I hoped that if some kid came and saw me, he or she would feel sorry for me. Maybe a vet could fix me up before I changed back to human form.

I didn't know if that was possible. All this supernatural stuff was still new to me. But I hoped I could get some medicine, at least.

But as the sky grew darker, I knew it was a lost cause. A lot of time had passed since I got off the school bus. I realized finally that it was after dinner. No kid was going to be walking through the field on a school night this late.

My only hope was that Tak would come looking for me at my house. With luck, he'd figure out what had happened. Then maybe he would find me here.

If I was still alive. I could feel myself sinking fast. Tak had said that the Cat People were all mortal. If I died when I was a cat, I would also die as a human. It was a horrible thought. But there was no escape. I was going to die.

I thought about my mom and my dad. It was terrible to leave them. They would be very sad. Dakota Rose would be very sad, too. I was her favorite brother.

Well, I was her only brother. But she'd still be sad.

One thing, at least, did cheer me up. I had saved my baby sister from the Bads. So at least I had done some good before my life ended.

I could feel my eyes starting to close. The night was coming on fast. Things that had been clear became blurry. All I could see were shadows. Far-off sounds blurred together. I could hear the wind in my ears. My head felt dizzier and dizzier.

My eyelids were heavier than cement. I tried to use my paw to keep them from closing, but I was too weak. With a last gasp, I felt my eyes close.

At that very second, the ground began to rumble beneath me. A howling rose up from far away. It sounded like a thousand wolves roaring at the moon.

A sweet smell filled my nostrils. It was a little like baked bread, fresh from the oven.

"You must eat this," said a gentle voice. "You have lost nearly all of your strength. If you don't eat, you will die."

I opened my eyes. A large white lion stood over me. He had two massive tusks, and a gray mane. His eyes glowed bright white. When he spoke, his voice was so deep the ground shook.

"Go on, Alan. It's OK."

"B-but Tak told me that if I eat while I'm in cat form, I will remain a cat forever," I muttered.

"That is true. But if you don't eat, you will die. It's your choice."

The lion took a step backward. For just a second I thought I saw a shadow in his face, something familiar. Was this my great-grandpa Al?

He glanced downward. A dead chipmunk lay right near my mouth.

I hesitated. Even though I had just beaten those three evil cats, I knew I wasn't really ready to join the cat spirits for good. I wanted to say good-bye to my parents, and to my sister, and to my friends at school. Even my teachers.

Plus, I had a tremendous amount to learn. I was just a kid. My great-grandfather had waited for many, many years before he joined the Cat People and their fight against evil.

But there was no other choice. I could feel my heart starting to fail. The beats were getting slower and slower, like a windup toy running down. The chipmunk was right in front of me. It smelled so good, so delicious.

If I ate it, I would never be with my parents or my sister as a boy again. They would think I'd disappeared, just like Grandpa Al did.

But what else could I do?

I leaned my head over, and started to chew.

17

And that is how I became a saber-toothed tiger. For all time. I even got a new name: Ahiga. It means "he who fights."

To be honest, it was very sad at first. My parents spent a year looking for me. I hung around the house for a long time, trying to convince them I was OK.

They didn't know it was me, though. All they saw was a tiger-striped pussy cat. Mom and Dad thought I was a lost pet. Oh, they were nice and all, but they couldn't keep me. My mom started sneezing every time I was in the room for more than ten minutes.

My sister wanted to keep me. She had seen me change into a cat. She tried to tell them and the police. No one knew exactly what to make of her story. They thought she was just confused. She finally had to give up trying to convince them.

Maybe someday, when she's older, Dakota Rose will find Grandpa Al's old book in my room. Mom tucked it in the bookcase. Everything is just like it was when I lived there. If Dakota reads it, she'll figure everything out.

But that's far in the future. I can't worry about that now. Every night, I roam the earth with the other good cats, seeking out the Bads. I've grown quite a bit since I first became a saber-toothed tiger. I've gotten a lot better at fighting. Nowadays, if I encountered three puny little Bads like Stinky and his pals, I'd whip them with one hand tied behind my back.

I mean, one paw behind my back.

There was one funny thing that happened. It turned out that Mrs. Johnson hadn't actually been eaten by the Bads at all. She'd gone on that trip with her sister just like the police thought. She had left her pocketbook in the house because she had gotten a brand new one the week before.

The cats had played around in her house after she had left. They must have been the ones who knocked over the bookcase. It turns out the Bads are pretty clumsy, not to mention slobs. So her disappearance was all a coincidence, I guess.

I don't see my great-grandpa that much. He's ruler of the Cat People now, and that means a lot of extra work. But every so often we get together for some fun.

The evil cats were right about one thing—good cats can't fly. But we do a couple of things that are even better.

I can't write about them, since we have to keep some secrets to ourselves. I'm not even allowed to say what happened to the amulet.

My great-grandfather gave me special permission to write this, in hopes that our next recruit will know what to expect. When that will be, no one knows. Maybe right now, someone is leaning down to pick up a strange stone in a field. He probably won't realize it has special powers. He won't even know it's an amulet. All he'll think is that it's a good luck charm.

He'll put it in his pocket. Sometime after that, he'll start to hear strange voices when no one's around. He may notice a stray cat hanging around that he's never seen before. One night, something will scratch at his window.

All he'll see will be an innocent little kitty cat, staring inside, curious.

That's when the fun will begin.